Return to the Grass

TNY Books, McCormick, SC

TNY Books
McCormick, SC

Published in the USA by TNY Books, 2022
Cover Design by TNY Media

Cover photo source: Dreamstime.com
Cover photo credits:
Grass background - Photo 121445519 © Leklek73;
Blood spatter - Photo 168992391 © Ilya Podoprigorov

ISBN: 9798218117085 (Paperback)
ISBN: 9798218117115(eBook)

Other Books by the Author:

Murder at Wimbledon
Fulton Books, 2022

Good Strokes for Senior Folks
The New You Publishing, 2020

Frozen in Time
The New You Publishing

Natural Tennis, 2nd Ed. With John Boaz
Stipes Publishing, 2010

Natural Movement for Children
Kendall-Hunt, 1982

Social and Emotional Development of Children
Canadian Association for HPERD, 197

Author's Note

When I finished Murder at Wimbledon, the story was clearly unfinished. It was then, after my editor insisted that I continue my adventure, that I started writing this sequel. As with the first book, much of the story I lived as a young man in the early 90's. I had made some short notes of those years at Wimbledon and beyond. I had forgotten about them until the COVID lockdown of 2020. It was only then that I had the time to write my first novel and start a second.

As there were no novels and only two or three fictional movies where tennis was a part of the main theme, I had little to guide my path. I was however inspired by two Alfred Hitchcock movies made in the 50's, to write something authentic and believable, set in a time and place that I had experienced. I was also inspired by the many friends and acquaintances I made during that time, any references to which in these pages are purely fictional.

Introduction

Jack Hardigan returns to London to continue his adventures. He hoped it would be another great summer in his favorite city where he would again try to qualify for Wimbledon. This time he had a formidable group of friends he could count on to help him through these unpredictable spring and summer months.

It was now the spring of 1992. A decade before this a successive influx of Arab and Russian money had swamped London's real estate market. The stylish new Bond Street and even Oxford Street had been upgraded by the likes of Burberry, Cartier, Chanel, and Hermes. Well-heeled tourists and locals alike flocked to the cool brand name stores and expensive restaurants and clubs. The area became too expensive for the old established stores and galleries. They moved out and the Russians and Poles moved in, with their nightclubs, casinos, and restaurants. Yuri Grosegann and his brother had acquired much of the best real estate in the west end. The Italians cornered the market in the east end. There were evenly defined territorial lines. Yuri Grosegann had amassed a small fortune controlling the liquor trade, real estate transactions, protection gambit, massage clubs and gambling.

Jack Hardigan got to know Grosegann after the death of his friend Dom Gloriosos, the Italian underworld boss, who was killed outside the main gate at Wimbledon. After some coaxing, I had started coaching Yuri's nephew, Michel, in tennis. He quickly became one of Britain's top juniors and had good prospects for the future with quality expert coaching.

Frank Brown, whom Jack had met two summers ago and had become close friends with last summer, would again be helping him navigate through the coming months. Predictably, there are several beautiful women back in Jack's life. This summer begins with a promise of a single man's cavorting and tennis, but quickly adds intrigue, violence and excitement on and off the grass courts. This summer Jack has promised to coach Michel Grosegann again, and get him ready for Junior Wimbledon, connecting him once again to the London underworld.

Frank has again arranged for Jack to give exhibitions and clinics as Slazenger's ambassador at some of the most luxurious country houses outside of London and in Scotland. Mirium, the beautiful, widowed diamond heiress meets Jack on his arrival and has him stay with her at her country estate, Winston Gardens. Here he can train with Frank and coach Michel on Mirium's private grass courts. Little does he know that Yuri has developed several new gangland rivals after the murder of Sicilian boss Dom Gloriosos. These ruthless and jealous opponents are anxious to take over London's gambling clubs, prostitution, and smuggling operations. Jack soon finds that he is constantly followed wherever he goes.

Susan too has been eagerly awaiting Jack's return. Susan, a woman to be remembered. An incredibly beautiful, yet very naïve, young lady, lacking any self-confidence, who defined herself by the man she was attached to. Jack met her through Dom Gloriosos, whom she was dating. Jack had stepped in to comfort her and she immediately latched on to him to fill the void left by Dom's death. Susan continues to work at Dom's club, now run by his younger alcoholic brother.

Joanne, another beautiful woman who Jack met in classes at London University is also eagerly awaiting Jack's return. She is a no-strings-attached type who is content to spend a few days with Jack when they are both in town.

Jack spends his first months in London preparing Michel to compete in Junior Wimbledon. Jack again plays through qualifying to make it into the main draw and again another dramatic Centre Court encounter, this time against the legendary Boris Becker.

A dead man's body is recovered just outside Yuri's club. It turns out he was an employee at the Russian Embassy, in other words, a Russian spy. As Jack Hardigan is now coaching Yuri Grosegann's nephew, he is informed about the case by Inspector O'Neill. The Russian spy, according to O'Neill, was found in possession of a pen containing a microchip, which a review by Scotland Yard and M15 showed as having the complete plans for the revamped London power grid. Inspector O'Neill's intent to thwart any planned attack on the city's infrastructure was going to take full advantage of the connections that Jack and his good friend, Frank Brown had to the Russian underworld. The three of them embark on a daring caper to flush out the spy ring behind this mystery plot.

The next week after Wimbledon, Mirium takes Jack to Lausanne, Switzerland for a short vacation. While there, they visit her Swiss Banker who takes them on a tour of Mirium's fine art collection held in a climate-controlled vault at the bank. These paintings were acquired by her deceased husband during his years operating his South African diamond mines. Jack and Mirium discover a little-known Van Gogh which has been hidden away for thirty years. It is worth at least 15 million US dollars. Jack and Mirium must decide on what to do with it before word of its discovery is leaked out to the world.

When Mirium's bank is moving her artwork to another facility, it is hijacked by a group of ruthless killers. Unfortunately, the priceless Van Gogh is one of those stolen. After this, Jack and Mirium set off on a dangerous odyssey to track down and recover the painting. From Switzerland to Italy, their travel begins to unwind a thread of power and corruption in a race to reach the stolen painting before it disappears forever.

Jack tells his story again with the same passion and empathy with his new friends in support. There is intrigue, jealousy, deception, violence, love and death and a few surprises, in this sequel that will not disappoint Jack Hardigan fans.

1

Back in London

My heart was pounding in my chest as my flight touched down at Heathrow. My expectations were high looking forward to a good summer and seeing my friends again. It's a long overnight flight from the west coast. Memories of last summer had been swimming through my mind, both in my thoughts when I was awake and in my dreams as I slept. At one point the stewardess woke me from what apparently was a nightmare, offering me a warm towel for my face. I was apparently thrashing in my sleep as if fighting off assailants. Perhaps memories of being abducted last year. Other than the fitful sleep on the plane, I felt pretty good about my situation. I had just graduated with my doctorate. My mother had showed up from Australia to see me graduate and we had a small party to celebrate. I said goodbye to all my friends and professors in Eugene and looked forward to a good trip to London. I was now free to pursue my life. I was looking forward to hooking up with my best friend on this side of the Big Pond, Frank. Of course, I had been dreaming about seeing Susan and Mirium, the two main women in my life in London, playing over in my mind how those reunions would go. Obviously, I was also looking forward to more time playing tennis on the pristine grass courts in England and the Wimbledon matches. Once again, I experienced that sensation I had last summer that my life was at one of those pivotal moments that redefines the direction you were heading. A sensation of uncertainty, adrenaline, and a touch of apprehension of the unknown.

I was alert and vigilant getting off the plane and moving through the airport, having learned from last year's episode of someone using me as a mule for incriminating paperwork regarding their assassination 'assignment', then breaking into my hotel room to retrieve it. It was early morning, and the terminal was full of businessmen and women as well as tourists and families trying to get an early start to their holiday.

Frank was to meet me outside baggage claim. Something about not wanting to park the car in a public lot. I grabbed a carrier for my baggage and took it outside to the curb, the damp, smog filled air causing me to cough suddenly, as the doors of the terminal opened. I would have to get used to this air again. I looked about for Frank, but he was not in sight. After a couple of minutes of watching every conceivable make and model of car pull up to pick up passengers, Frank suddenly appeared before me and said, "What are you waiting for, a bus?" I turned and looked along the curb for his car as he walked a few steps ahead of me, turned and introduced me to his new maroon Bentley. I was more than a little impressed. "Business must be very good", I said, as the trunk silently opened on its own. "Been saving for a while!" was his response as we loaded my luggage.

One thing you need to understand is that Frank was a very savvy businessman. He had built a very successful chain of sports stores in England, using money he had mostly borrowed from some of the wrong type of people. One of the adventures last summer, was making sure that those debts got paid off. He was now free and clear, and he had great connections in all the right places for a businessman. Now he re-invests his profits into growing his business, and, judging by this latest toy, also into a few creature comforts. He lived a very comfortable lifestyle for a single 36-year-old, surrounding himself with a few nice things and supporting his, not surprising, penchant for beautiful women. Despite being one of London's more eligible bachelors, in his own words, when we first met, he "preferred to be very selective in his choices when it came to women". Truth was, he was not what most women would call "handsome", not bad looking, just not the type to stand out in a crowd. He did, however, have an amazing ability to get women to adore him, basically, just by the way he listened when they spoke. It was somewhat uncanny the way women gravitated to him at parties.

While I was away in the States, Frank had upped his level of living. Life was good for him – his hard work and perseverance had paid off. His friends and business associates respected his ambition and determination, and they trusted him. Frank seemed very committed to helping others. He had recently talked Uri into supporting some of his charities. Even before I returned back he had me signed up to do three free clinics with Slazenger in the poorer section of East London. As I had gotten to know him, I found him to be a very honest and stable person with a lust for travel now that he was wealthy enough to enjoy first-class travel. He was a very good county tennis player, was a member of Queens' club, and could have been a pro had he had the time to pursue it when he was younger.

I slid into the front seat, and it felt as if it had been molded just for my jet lagged and aching body. I had to struggle not to fall asleep before clicking my seat belt. It felt amazing to be able to stretch my legs out to their full length. I hadn't realized just how tense I was. With Frank, I felt comfortable and safe. He drove through heavy traffic, back to one of several condos which he had purchased as investments. Despite his constant chatter, I believe I dozed off several times. We got to his place, which I recognized as the one in Kensington which he was having extensive renovations and updates done to last year. I was only vaguely aware of my surroundings as I unpacked some of the more essential items and clothes, then collapsed onto the bed for a long, dreamless nap.

Frank had said he had some errands to run and would wake me when he got back. I managed to sleep for about three hours and was feeling much better when he woke me. I took a quick shower, organized some of my clothes and we headed out to lunch at our favorite coffee shop. As we sat down and ordered, I felt so at home it was hard to believe I had been gone for over half a year. He only had time for a quick lunch, but he did let me know that Yuri wanted to see me, and that I should see him first thing tomorrow morning. "I guess he wants to get first dibs on my time to be sure I continue working with his nephew" I commented with a broad grin, remembering how well he pays me to coach his nephew in tennis.

We walked back towards his condo and parted ways as we got close. He had chosen this particular location to live in since it was close to the tube, which he used often in preference over trying to navigate through London traffic. His business kept him busy with meetings that he couldn't afford to be late to. He had given me a key to his place, and I returned for a bit more sleep. As I entered the lobby through the heavy revolving glass doors, I spotted a security guard at a desk which I hadn't noticed earlier. I assumed that he hadn't made any notice of me since I was with Frank. I walked over and was impressed by the array of security monitors surrounding him, discreetly hidden behind the counter I had approached. He handed me a security key card with my picture already on it to be used for the elevators. He smiled at my surprise and pointed to one of the monitors that was aimed at the front doors, and which snapped a photo of anyone entering. He said I would need it to verify my identity to the other guards on different shifts. I took a lift to Frank's third floor unit, shaking my head at how much the world was changing that made security like this necessary for a residential building. I finished unpacking and wandered around the very nicely furnished and comfortable domicile. Frank either had very good taste when funds were at his disposal, or he hired a very good decorator. Either way, I easily found the bar, poured myself a short bourbon and settled into one of the recliners that offered a view through his balcony doors, overlooking the area around Kensington Park. As I lay back in the chair I was thinking that this was going to be the best summer ever. I had barely taken a sip of my drink when I drifted off into a peaceful sleep.

By the time Frank returned I was just waking from my sleep. He put his papers down, kicked off his shoes, loosened his tie and poured himself a drink to match mine. "So, what do you think?" he asked as he indicated the surroundings with a swipe of his head. "I could make do" was my response, feigning a haughty smirk. He grabbed a shoe as if to throw it at me, then laughed as he claimed that "Upscale surroundings always did suit you." Upscale was a very accurate description of this place. Though from outside it appeared to be situated in a single older brownstone, in reality it spanned four such buildings. There was a large sunken living room which sufficed for entertaining his clients a few times a year. For larger parties during the more pleasant spring and autumn weather, steps lead up to large glass sliders which opened to a rooftop patio garden, partially protected from hot sun or light rain by shade sails, with decorative strings of lights for evening illumination. One corner of the living room was raised and furnished with bookshelves and two chairs flanking a large, marble chess set, set off by several large house plants, giving the illusion of an outdoor park. I could easily imagine Frank sitting opposite one of his chess buddies as they went head-to-head for hours on end. It seems that Frank's parties had become somewhat legendary, partly due to his enchanting venue, but also due to his eclectic guest lists. After last summer's events, it was not surprising to see attendees from all levels of London's social scenes, from the latest hot celebs and models to political figures, to nightclub owners and 'suspected' crime syndicate bosses.

We headed out for a few beers before dinner, which gave us time to catch up and discuss our summer schedule. We were planning on the usual exhibitions, clinics, and demos of Slazenger's latest line of tennis gear. We hoped to get most of these scheduled early on so I could relax the remainder of the summer, while dedicating time to looking towards my future. A topic which I have been sorely remiss in addressing. Of course, there was also the time needed to prepare for the Wimbledon

Tournaments. That was one of the main reasons for the exhibition with Slazenger's new equipment. I have always believed the best way to practice is by mimicking real life play. What better way than in actual matches on grass courts.

Mirium had called me on my arrival at Frank's saying how much she had missed me and that she looked forward to seeing me soon at Winston Gardens. We decided that I would stay with Frank for the first few days in London and then head off to Mirium's after that. I had entered the main Wimbledon qualifying events via my Australian Federation, at Nottingham, Eastbourne, Frinton and Queens. I had entered the doubles with Michel as my partner. Playing in the Open doubles would be a great experience for him. I was hopeful he was up to it. We would train at Winston Gardens when not in qualifying events. When in London Frank had activated my Queens Club membership so we could practice on the best grass courts, and I could easily arrange practice matches for Michel. I also had three major exhibitions planned through Slazenger. Phew! Otherwise, my time was my own. However, much of my commitment was self-inflicted as I loved what I was doing and the summertime in England. In the Northern Hemisphere, the days gradually got longer into the spring and summer. It seemed everyone looked forward to these long days of sunshine. The women all started to wear their short dresses, showing more skin. The early 90's London fashion scene saw miniskirts being replaced with micro-minis. Since cell phones were nonexistent as was social media at this time, the women were more interested in catching the eye of a potential suitor than staring at their phones, so it was easier for males to get and keep their attention. My mind was jetlagged, so by the time we sat down for dinner, comments on the attire (or seeming lack thereof) of the ladies in the establishment was about the extent of my conversation. Frank had gotten up unusually early to retrieve me at the airport, followed by running around playing host to me and still keeping up with business. We were both content to return to his condo and turn in after dinner.

I awoke bright and early the next day, still trying to adjust to the time change, and I showed up early to meet with Yuri Grosegann, London's Russian West End casino owner, who had asked to meet with me.

We met at our usual spot, one of his clubs. The heavy girl behind the bar dropped her magazine and delivered two coffees to our table. Yuri's an espresso, mine, a cappuccino. His personal bodyguard, Max had taken up a discrete position near the front entrance. I noticed a large ruby ring on Yuri's left hand. He had one finger missing on his right. Yuri knew just about everything that was going on in London's business world and all the local criminals and their dealings. He was the undisputed king of London's underworld now that Dom Gloriosos, my friend, had been killed last summer, outside the main gate at Wimbledon. Without a word he reached inside his coat pocket and handed me an envelope containing 4,000 pounds in large notes to be a first payment, he said, "to use for my expenses". We had agreed last year that I would continue to work with his nephew, Michel and get him ready for junior Wimbledon. He said he liked what I did last summer, and he was hopeful of not only success on the tennis court but also helping Michel avoid the usual troubles of teenage boys, as he called it, "temptations of the flesh". Considering my own antics, I'm not sure I qualified as a stellar example of self-control, but I didn't see a need to argue with Yuri.

Max Mulligan, Yuri's bodyguard, was a small-time hood, who respected me because of my close friendship with his old boss, Dom. Mulligan, had he not been a gangster, would have been quite at home breaking up boulders on the nearby prison yard. He had not been to prison yet but had been close. He had been endowed with bulging muscles which gave him a tough intimidating appearance. However, he was very street smart and could be persuasive and devious when called for. He let me know, in no uncertain terms, that he would do anything for me. He was very protective of Michel and had specific instructions from Yuri to keep a watchful eye on both of us. Whenever Michel travelled, Yuri had him travel with an armed driver. Kidnappings had increased in London since I was taken by the Irish rebels last year. The Irish were still a threat, although many of those responsible for the bombings last year had been arrested and were going through the court system. Yuri's main threat in London was the Polish connection who had become more active in smuggling and prostitution, trying to take over the Sicilian's territory after the void left by Dom's death.

I could hear the street noise as the door of the empty club opened behind me. Yuri glanced in that direction and then motioned to Max to go to whoever it was who had interrupted our time together. I couldn't make out what was being said, but the tone was not friendly. I heard the door open again as the intruder left. Yuri looked questioningly at Max as he was returning to us and his gaze must have been met with some indication of the reason for the intrusion, since Yuri muttered some words I recognized as swearing. I thought I heard something that sounded like 'Polish' in the string of expletives. Yuri got up and excused himself with "Take good care of my nephew!".

I finished the last sip of my cappuccino and stepped out into the overcast mid-morning rush of London's metropolis. I had some free time before meeting up with Frank again to get together with one of London's renowned investigative journalists at 1:00 pm.

Byron Mortimer lived in a quiet end of West Kensington, so it was an easy walk from Queen's for Frank and me to meet him at his flat. Mortimer's newspaper stories had earned him a lot of enemies, some of whom wanted him dead. Mortimer was the reporter who broke the story when I punched out the murderer at Centre Court last summer and wrote a detailed three-part series about crime in London, including an expose on Dom Gloriosos and his associates after Dom's death. He also detailed the lives of Yuri Grosegann and the Russian connection as well as the rise of the ruthless Polish gangsters making moves into new territory for gambling clubs, bookmaking, prostitution, smuggling and more recently the growing drug trade. Mortimer was waiting for us on the landing outside his apartment. He had been adamant that he needed to see us. He drew us into his place with much enthusiasm. It was clear that this was the home of a writer, a successful one at that. Every flat surface was piled high with papers and books. He apologized for his clutter. He had recently been hired by the BBC to comment on crime in London and security preparations for Wimbledon.

He had a small corner studio, complete with video cameras, flood lighting and interview chairs. He considered me as a prime interviewee for his next story. We told him in advance that we hadn't much time to talk so as to limit the time we were there. He said he "had just a few questions I'd like to ask you, Jack".

Mortimer had recently just written a nasty piece about Dom's brother who had taken over from the deceased Dominique Gloriosos. He next asked a couple of probing questions about Yuri's nephew, Michel. I told him that, "Yuri was a good friend to both Frank and I and our relationship was limited to that friendship and only that friendship. Our friendship did not extend any further and had nothing to do with his other interests". When we ascertained where this was going, we decided to make our exit. However, the interview was actually great publicity for Frank's sports businesses in London. We drew attention to both Dom's and Yuri's grants and investments to various poor neighborhoods. We also made sure Byron would advertise our free kid's clinic in London's east end.

Actually, Yuri was very pleased that we did the interview when he saw it that night. The BBC showed video of Michel and I practicing at Queen's, using it as a promo for his articles on crime in London and about the latest Wimbledon security. The fact that I was the one that helped capture the notorious Irish bomber and crime boss, Sean McNeece was prominent in the piece.

2

And So It Begins

The evening was cool and dry. One of the few pleasant ones before summer really sets in. I had arranged to meet Susan for dinner. I was looking forward to seeing her and she was clearly delighted to be out with me. I had forgotten just how young and beautiful she was. We went out to a relaxed dinner at our favorite Italian bistro, Roma, just two blocks from the flat where she lived. I didn't care too much for the waiter. He was a bit overzealous. He had no sense of the rhythm of the meal and always seemed to be interrupting our talk. I suspect he just wanted to get a better look at Susan and enjoy her intoxicating perfume. I recognized it as "Passion" by Elizabeth Taylor. However, distracted he was, he did know his wines and the food was outstanding. Susan ordered Insalata Caprese and a light Bolognese. I had a Caesar salad and a large veal chop, the house specialty with a wild mushroom burgundy sauce, accompanied by a Pino Noir from the Umbria region. I do appreciate that in England, chefs don't try to make everything taste like English food, but, instead, provide authentic ethnic cuisine.

The last of her Pinot Noir reflected in the sublime candlelight. Her beautiful blue eyes focused on me directly. Susan appeared to have matured and grown up in the many months since I had seen her last. She seemed more independent. She was no longer the clingy, needy 'little girl' she was after the death of her mob-boss boyfriend last year. She said how much "she had missed me and that she had thought of me every day that I was away". She already knew about my relationship with Mirium which she never mentioned and was content to enjoy her time with me, when it did happen. I still had the key to her flat that she gave me last summer and she encouraged me to use it whenever I wanted to see her.

As we got near the end of our meal, she cast her eyes downward as she picked at the remains of her dinner. "I am so glad you are back in my life" and "I want to be part of yours whatever that may be" she said in a wavering voice. She made it clear that she loved me, even if she had to share that with someone else. Not knowing exactly what to say, I called the waiter over and we ordered a Tiramisu to share over coffee and Port. I took the first forkful and lovingly put it towards her lips as a silent commitment of my affection.

I was momentarily distracted by the man who entered as the waiters were clearing tables near the street windows. He stared directly at our table as he moved to take a seat in the shadows near the windows. From what I could tell, he looked to be Italian, maybe Sicilian, with a deep olive coloured complexion. He was wearing a brown bomber jacket and had a large scar across his left cheek. He made no attempt to hide the fact that he was looking our way. He also seemed preoccupied with Susan, taking in every inch of her as his eyes moved from her feet up along her slender but shapely legs and hips, to her ample and youthful breasts, her long slender neck and finally her flawless face and hair. I was about to get out of my seat and confront his blatant lack of respect when Susan's hand touched mine and brought me back to our conversation.

We continued with small talk about how our lives were going as we finished our dessert. As the waiter handed me the cheque, I glanced over to the window seat and the man I had seen before was gone and an elderly couple was being seated there. I couldn't shake the feeling that there was more to his presence than a voyeuristic attraction to Susan. All things considered, it was a wonderful evening and a great way to clear the air and set our ground rules for our relationship. That had been a great suggestion made by Frank, to be honest about it and enjoy both women without strings attached and without hurting anyone. At this point I felt very lucky and flattered to have both Mirium and Susan caring for me. However, Frank promised that he would keep them apart if they showed up on the same day. This could be a challenge. After dinner we danced a bit and then walked back to her flat. Susan immediately took me back to her bedroom where I was reminded of her athleticism from spending her nights as a dancer at a club. We made passionate love 'til early morning.

Walking back to Frank's on London's backstreets, at this time of night, there's a whiff of sewerage in the air. It wasn't quite late enough for first light, but some birds were just beginning to awaken with soft song, as if practicing for the coming dawn. As I cross the street, I catch a glimpse of a tall, skinny man in a dark suit ducking into the shelter of a shadowy doorway. After I was on the other side, I looked back and decided that it had just been shadows from the streetlights playing tricks on my eyes and there was nobody there after all. I guess that the adventures of last year had left a small scar of paranoia, which was fueling my imagination. I put it out of my mind and made a mental note to stop imagining things.

I tried to be as quiet as I could entering Frank's apartment, but he apparently heard the door latch. He donned a robe and put on some coffee. We sat there in the semi dark, discussing how we would deal with both women and how I could be with both, without hurting either. He got up and came back with two cups of coffee. As we sat sipping the hot coffee, Frank was tapping the side of his mug with his finger. He finally gave me a piercing look and pointed out the obvious. "You know you're going to have to make some decisions about Mirium and Susan." I scowled at him, knowing full well that he was right. "In a perfect world I could love two women." I lamented. According to sixteenth century philosopher, Voltaire 'perfection is the enemy of love' and love can easily become lost without proper nurturing. "Time will tell", I said. In reality, my needs at the moment were very simple, and all I wanted was to 'go with the flow' without hurting anyone. In retrospect, a very shallow and selfish attitude. "I am very lucky to have two great women".

The next day, Frank and I met Michel at Queen's Club and had a good practice. While I was away Michel had grown two inches and filled out in the chest and shoulders. He had grown into the robust physique of an athletic male and had obviously been working on the techniques I had taught him last year during our brief practice time toward the end of my trip. He had also spent time developing the muscles necessary for a strong game. His potential was obvious and if I didn't make the cut for the men's draw at Wimbledon, I would devote my full attention to coaching Michel.

It was good to be back practicing on the grass again. This was my favorite playing surface, although I had had some good wins recently winning the Pacific Western and the Pacific Southwest doubles as a part time player against some stiff West Coast opposition. The fast hard courts suited my serve and volley game as did grass. Just smelling the grass was addictive, but the bounce on the grass was more unpredictable. I could tell I would need time to adjust again to the slick grass courts of qualifying and Wimbledon.

O'Neill, our friend from Scotland Yard had called Frank's place earlier, to welcome me back to London. Thinking this was nothing more than a social visit, I arranged to meet him at a local corner pub after practice and a shower. He was there as I entered and greeted me as I approached the bar where he was sitting. He got up and offered his hand in a welcoming handshake. "You're looking well", said O'Neill. "Being back in London obviously agrees with you". I asked, "How did you know I was here?" "There isn't much that happens in London that I don't know about." He replied with a grin and a wink. We went around the side of the bar to a backroom which was more private and had its own smaller bar. O'Neill ushered me to a corner table and quickly pulled out a single 8x10 photograph which he placed on the table in front of me. I sat there in horror as I looked at the photo, wondering why he was sharing this with me. It showed a young athletic looking man hanging, half naked, from a doorway by his wrists. The body was covered in bruises and wounds that indicated the man had been brutally beaten and tortured. The face was an unrecognizable mass of blood and pulverized flesh. The legs hung at unnatural angles from obviously broken bones. The fatal blow was a knife cut across his abdomen which exposed his bowels. The body was found by Italian police on an estate on Lake Garda. According to O'Neill his name was Roger Randall a British tennis player. The blood drained from my face and my stomach wretched. This was the man I had played last year at Wimbledon on Centre Court. My mind was reeling. Why would Roger have been tortured and murdered in such a gruesome fashion? What could he have possibly been involved in that could get him so brutally murdered? Whatever it was, he was definitely left as a statement warning other not to mess with whatever group did this. I pushed the picture back towards O'Neill to get it out of my sight. Unfortunately, I don't think I will ever be able to expunge it from my memory.

Once my mind stopped reeling from the graphic photo, and I was able to get the lump out of my throat and speak, I started asking the obvious questions. Was Roger in debt, was he involved in gambling, the underworld, or drugs? Who was his significant other, wife, girlfriends? What was he doing in Italy? O'Neill said 'he was completely in the dark' as to the whole case and this is why he was asking us for help. Right now, it was all speculation as to what had happened to Roger and why he was in Italy. Roger was a handsome bachelor with a roving eye. He had lots of pretty women, played the ponies, gambled and did pretty much as he pleased. His father was wealthy and owned a string of expensive racehorses and had business associates in London's underworld. Roger was not a saint, but his father thought he could do no wrong and was pleased that his son had become one of Britain's top tennis players. O'Neill asked if he could include Frank and I on a committee of inquiry as we knew Roger and could certainly help the police with information on this crime. I immediately agreed and though I couldn't speak for Frank, I was sure he would be willing to help out.

Frank was waiting for me as I left the pub. My gate was still faltering a bit from the memory of that picture and my ashen complexion was obvious in the light of day. I hesitated before opening the car door to take a deep breath. He was leaning over to see my face and, when I finally opened the door to get in, immediately asked "What the hell happened? Are you OK? Did something happen to Mirium?" "Mirium is fine," I said. He sat in silence as I filled him in on my conversation with O'Neill, describing the photo I had been shown. My voice began to falter as I recalled what I had seen. After a few moments of silence while I regained my composure again, I told him that O'Neill has asked for our involvement on a committee of inquiry. Without hesitation, he agreed to help in any way he could and asked me to pass that on to O'Neill. We rode along in silence, both lost in our own thoughts, filled with questions. Traffic was thankfully light, as I'm not sure how much Frank was focused on driving. He managed to drop me at the station just in time for me to catch the four o'clock to Winston Gardens.

Mirium was at the station to greet me in her new maroon Jaguar. I had managed to quell my response to the earlier events and put on a 'happy' face as I got off the train and approached the car. The sight of her helped to push aside the memory of my conversation with O'Neill, and my smile was genuine. Her sublime grace and beauty were enough to bring the colour back to my face. She was obviously glad to see me, fussing over me, and telling me of her plans for tonight and the next few days. As we drove up her estate driveway to the main house, I felt as if I had come home. As we walked beside each other on the way to the front doors, we were illuminated by the soft glow of the sun as it lowered toward the horizon. I caught a glimpse of our reflection in the terrace windows. I had to admit, with me in my clean white shirt and Mirium in her black slacks, blue blouse and Pierre

Cardin, leather vest, we looked like a very attractive couple. We went on into the house, it was cool and inviting with fresh flowers everywhere. She flung her arms about my neck. I could feel she was trembling with anticipation and excitement. Her butler took my bags with an almost imperceivable grin and raised eyebrow. We sat down for a drink. She talked and I listened as we waited for supper to be prepared. She stopped mid-sentence and apologized for rambling, but there was so much she wanted to share with me. I laughed and told her "No worries, I love listening to your voice. I truly missed it." Thankfully, she had a nice quiet dinner planned, served up by her local part time French chef. "I'm not very good at being alone, especially since I met you Jack. Since you have been away, I have missed you terribly. I need you Jack".

After a nice simple dinner, we talked for a long time. She wanted to know everything about my time back in the states. She had been very disappointed that she was unable to attend my graduation, as she had planned. Her friend's husband, who had suffered a heart attack last summer while I was there, had a second one, and this time he needed bypass surgery. She just wasn't able to get away. Her friend needed her to be there. We talked about her hopes for the summer and things she had been waiting to do with me.

3

Back At Winston Gardens

I showered and unpacked and collapsed onto the bed. It was familiar, had a feeling of home. A rush of memories from last season flooded my mind and reached my loin. I opened my eyes to see Mirium, like a vision, naked in her perfect body, coming to me with the look of a tigress ready to pounce. We were on each other as primitive animals in heat. It had been many months. Our thirst for each other seemed unquenchable. We were wrestling for position, rolling around, entwining our bodies, trying to get every inch of our beings touching. Trying to become one. One moment tightly squeezing and biting, then another taking the time to caress and adore, as our bodies road the wave of our surging desires. The final crescendo coming when we could hold off no more. She was hovering over me and with one final thrust down, I let go and it felt as if the world had just split wide open and I was filling an endless void. Her orgasm, squeezing life from me for what seemed like forever. We reluctantly separated, panting, sweating, breathless, exhausted. Before she collapsed next to me I caught a glimpse of, the moonlight from our window casting her elegant profile on the wall, with her perfectly proportioned face and her long slender neck, and her full and rounded breasts, all caught in a beautiful silhouette. She kissed me softly on my chest, sending a shiver of delight through my body as I slipped into a deep sleep. There was a sensation as if I had been propelled into a different dimension, a different world. I was suddenly back in Oregon on my last night before leaving. We were all gathered at our favorite watering hole in Eugene, the Paddock. My Oregon mates and other graduates had gathered there as we usually did at the end of the week to tell our stories, swap exam papers, class notes, opinions of our professors, and share all this with wives and girlfriends. In my dream, my friend, Steve Prefontaine, world distance runner record holder, was there serving beers as he had done before his tragic death on Skinner's Butte some years before this. My dream though was reliving my farewell, the day before I was to catch my flight for Los Angeles, and then a British Airlines flight for London. On my arm at our table was my Oregon student sweetheart, Cindy. After a few beers we all decided to head out to the Laurelwood Country Club, as we often did, which had a dance floor and a disc jockey on Friday nights. We could all dance with our girls there to our favorite music, tell more stories and have a few more drinks. The dream ended with a finality that underscored the end of a chapter in my life. I knew at that moment that nothing would ever be the same.

The birds outside our window woke us. The garden was covered with dew and there was a slight mist in the air. It was good to be back. We decided we would go riding around the estate this morning and I had Michel coming in the afternoon for training on Mirium's grass courts. She had her grounds man specially working on them in anticipation for our practices. Mirium was very excited to show me off and for me to meet some of her friends. She was organizing a cocktail party for the next week and asked what night would be best for me. Monday, Tuesday and Wednesday were good, but I had to head back into London for the remainder of the week, returning on Monday. She briefly became solemn at the thought of me being away again so soon, but quickly recovered with a slightly nervous voice, saying, "Monday, it is then!" I am certain that she remembered last summer when I was seeing 'someone else' on occasion. I took her in my arms and softly kissed her full red lips and held her close for a moment, while I whispered, "I won't be away for long." I also mentioned that I needed to schedule a recording of a television interview with Byron Mortimer. I told Mirium that we could do the interview by the courts at Winston, showing off her beautiful courts and gardens. Of course, there was Wimbledon Qualifying with Michel and Mirium wanted to do Ascot, plus she wanted to be with me when I was to interview at Oxford. She also brought up a trip to meet with her Banker in Lausanne, Switzerland that she was hoping I could fit into my schedule. Just a day trip. Apparently there was some artwork left by her late husband in storage at the bank, and she wanted to see what was there. That could be after Wimbledon and she was thinking it would be a great opportunity, as we could make the trip into a nice vacation, maybe from there take a relaxing train ride to Venice, then Rome and the Italian Riviera as a reward for my diligent studies. Sounded great to me!

Michel arrived in a classic black limo, driven by his uncle's employee, Alex, who doubles as a bodyguard whenever he makes the trip up to Winston Garden. There was too much tension in the underworld as different factions vied for power, for Yuri to leave his nephew unguarded and exposed. The practice was a bit grueling, but I was trying to give Michel a feel for the pressure that he would face in a match at Wimbledon. Mirium had actually spent the afternoon with one of her friends in a town close by and didn't get back until late. The cook was gracious enough to prepare a light supper for me. As she removed my empty plate, she hesitated a bit and then said, "Please forgive me for being forward, but I have known Miss Mirium for a very long time, and care deeply for her as a very fine person. I think you should know how much she has changed in the time she has known you. You have made her to love life again. I just wanted to thank you for that." Her cheeks turned a deep red as she quickly turned and left the room.

Mirium had two reserved tickets at the Royal Albert Hall to see Tom Jones in Concert the next day. We planned to make it a day in London. The show was a 1pm matinee, sold out for months, so we had lots of time. We felt good to be together again, planned to do some London shopping then afternoon tea at the Ritz. As we entered the building I noticed a tall dark man in the shadows, well groomed, well dressed and a relaxed, confident air about him. He appeared to be watching us. Might have been plain clothes security, or just someone admiring Mirium. Or something else? After last year's seemingly constant cloak and dagger situations I was still a bit inclined to jump to conclusions. The murder of Roger did nothing to help me feel safe and secure.

We arrived early; traffic was light. We had time for a coffee before the show. We found a small table in the lobby, near the bar. I looked into Mirium's eyes. I loved her eyes-the way she looked back at me, as though she was looking into my brain, I just being in her company was like a small glimpse of heaven. "Tell me about your winters at Winston Gardens". "What do you do with yourself?" I asked. "Oh, I have my foundation and my work helping with fundraising for the orphanage, but I do get lonely by myself. When the weather gets miserable, I usually go to my apartment in St Tropez, or fly off to my favorite out of the way resort in Jamaica, well away from tourists. There are also friends that I enjoy visiting with, or spending a day with, in London enjoying the many restaurants and venues. Sometimes, I just sit down and get lost in a book."

The curtain call bell rang, and we made our way with others upstairs to our seats. We marveled at the magnificent circular building, the wall carvings, décor and lighting and of course the well-dressed crowd of patrons around us. When Tom Jones came out on stage, the crowd erupted in unison. As one might expect, the audience was captivated as Tom Jones warbled into "I'll never Fall in Love Again" and "It's Not Unusual". He then hit the high notes of "Thunderball" and the "Green, Green Grass of Home". He regaled us with his stories about his longtime friendship with Elvis and Priscilla. He was obviously very at home on the stage. He had sold over 100 million records, always performing on stage with his notable easy flowing manner. When he sang 'Delilah' everyone rose up, then after a few verses started singing with him. It was just extraordinary. He continued for two hours, sharing stories with the crowd about growing up in Wales and about his world travels and performing most of his favorites. We felt privileged to be there.

After the show we window shopped, and I bought a nice Harris Tweed sports coat and a new tuxedo at Burberry's. They took all my measurements and said now I could write or call them and order from anywhere in the world in the future. We walked to the Ritz for afternoon tea. The tall man with the dark suit was walking in the same direction, however, he easily could have been any of the tourists or locals out for a leisurely after show stroll, stopping occasionally for window shopping, sipping a coffee as he walked. I never got a good look at his face, but I took note of his build and posture. Afternoon Tea at the Ritz is a special tradition which Mirium wanted me to experience. After tea we had a cab called and waiting for us from a side entrance. We quickly made it back to our parked car and had an easy uneventful drive back to Winston Gardens. I looked forward to seeing Frank and working with Michel on Mirium's grass courts the next day.

Dinner was ready shortly after we arrived back at Mirium's. As we finished eating, I rose and picked up the unfinished bottle of wine and two clean glasses. With a slight grin and a wink in her direction, Mirium flushed and giggled and rose from her seat. I slightly cocked my head in the general direction of the bedroom, with a "Ladies first". As she passed, she lightly brushed against me and used her most seductive walk to lead the way. It was going to be a very good night.

When I stepped outside the next morning, Michel was already out on the courts practicing his serve his bodyguard not far off. The courts had been freshly mown and rolled. The grass smelled so good. The late morning was crisp and cool. Michel had gotten stronger and had improved his serve in my absence. My message to him for the summer was "To be yourself, swing your swing. Don't try to copy anyone else's swing. Swing your own natural swing". After our practice I had to scurry off as Mirium had invited guests coming at 5pm for an 'informal' cocktail party on the terrace.

After a spell in Mirium steam bath, a soak in the tub and a shower, I finally felt up to getting dressed and showing my smiling face downstairs. I could hear that a few guests had arrived exactly on time. Some Brits were still sticklers about timeliness. As I was chatting with Mirium's neighbor, who had noted my presence last summer and was very curious about my reappearance this year, a man with dark black eyes was ushered in, who had some kind of injury to the right side of his face, scarred, pitted, and rigid compared to his left side. His right ear was missing. His hair was a gunmetal gray, which, along with his surreal face apparently made him ruggedly attractive to some women who liked seasoned, distorted looks in males. Several of the female guests seemed drawn to him. According to Frank "he seemed to arouse animal instincts in some women and also in a few men".

I'm not sure why, but personally, I found the injuries disturbing, they made me feel very uncomfortable. I decided to give him a wide berth at the party, moving away from him whenever I could. After several deft avoidance maneuvers, exchanging pleasantries with other guests, he cornered me. He handed me a glass of champaign saying, "I hear you were good friends with Dom Gloriosos". "Yes, I said, "he was one of my best friends in London-was always hospitable to Frank and me, introducing me to many great contacts. He enjoyed showing up at my tennis matches and entertaining us on his boat and at his club." "Were you at his funeral?" It all came out with too much cynicism, but that's how I felt. It was hard to hide my emotions about Dom. After all he was gunned down just a few months ago, right next to me, outside the main gate at Wimbledon.

He said his name was Stephenson and he spoke with an affected Cambridge accent, with his nose in the air as though he was sniffing snuff or something. When he spoke, it seemed he had a plum in his mouth. I said to myself, "this guy is some weird character". Turns out, he was a high official in the foreign office, as explained by Frank afterwards. Apparently, he had got his injuries in one of the bombings in Ulster. It had taken him a year to recover.

Frank said he was a quite tolerable chap and would be useful if we ever had foreign visa problems. Frank also said to be careful with him. Seems many suspected that he may be a Russian agent. Maybe Yuri would know more about him.

Suddenly a very tall, blonde woman appeared in front of me. She introduced herself as Ludmilla. She spoke with a slightly Russian accent. I had never met this woman before, but she took my hand in both of hers, and pressed it to her heart, as if we were old friends. I presumed she had recognized me from what had happened at Wimbledon last summer, when I punched out a killer on national TV. I'm thinking to myself, "I guess this is what happens at cocktail parties". Women do find athletic displays erotic. She noticed Mirium heading in my direction and disappeared as quickly as she appeared.

Mirium was gliding around the room, looking very elegant as usual. She was wearing a long cocktail dress that could bring sight to a blind man. It was white with the look of silk draped over the body of a goddess, low cut in front and back with a long split up the side. She came over to me, took my hand and introduced me all around to her friends, some of whom I had met before and a few who were getting quite drunk. Of course, most of the talk was about the gruesome, untimely murder of Roger Randall. The details were in all the papers and on the telly adding fuel and fervor to all the talk. Frank and I were baffled by it all, and we looked forward to our next meeting with O'Neill.

I felt unnerved by the brutal murder of Roger in Milan. That next night Mirium and I decided to get our minds off the murder. We drove from the house about twenty minutes to a simple Italian family restaurant called Peperino's. It was a weeknight and nearly deserted. The owner, Tony and his wife obviously knew Mirium and was grateful for our business. We ordered a bottle of northern Italian Prosecco, which came highly recommended by the owner's wife, who acted as the server in the restaurant on slow evenings, it was a perfect complement to our starter of antipasto and salad.

We sampled the homemade pastas which the owner took special pride in, claiming a 'secret family recipe' and followed with a veal chop large enough for us to share. We washed it down with a classic vintage Brunello. After some discussion about how pleasant it is to be out of the criminal limelight, we decided to just let the authorities handle the murder so we could put it out of our minds.

4

What Russian Spy?

We headed out along the old dirt road towards the distant green hills. It was great to fill my lungs with fresh country air. We let our mounts pick up speed. They obviously knew where they were going. I tell myself, "I could get used to this". Mirium is a fine equestrian. I am just a bit of a hack, but, I'm learning with Mirium's willing help.

The breeze picked up as we headed back to the house for drinks and dinner and some quiet time together. I was scheduled to meet with Frank and spend some time at the Slazenger headquarters first thing in the morning and then meet Michel at Queen's again for practice. We had an event at the Australian Embassy on Sunday. I felt bad leaving Mirium after only a few days back, but Frank and I had a meeting at Scotland Yard with O'Neill, which could take a while. It was only a few days, and I would stay with Frank, then catch the train back to Winston Gardens when my business was done with in London.

Frank was waiting for me as I got off the early morning commuter train. The station was wall to wall with people from every walk of life, all getting ready to start the daily ritual of working for a living. With my schedule today, I definitely felt like I fit right in. I worked my way towards the exits, in unison with the crowd.

As I passed through the doors, I was disheartened by the weather. A line of wet cabs in single file lined up against the curb under a black sky on Oxford Street. There was a constant misty drizzle. As Frank caught my gaze, he could read the disappointment on my face and informed me that the forecast was for this to continue for the rest of the day. I called Michel and told him to go for a run and hit the gym. There would be no grass court practice today. That actually worked out well. Frank had gotten a call earlier asking if our appointment at Slazenger could be a bit later in the morning. We had time for an unhurried cup of coffee and idle conversation.

Because of the morning traffic congestion, the easiest way for us to get to Slazenger was to take a cab. The Slazenger headquarters lay in a large old five-story warehouse in the antiquated industrial section of east London. It was close enough to the docks for easy import and export of products. Most of their tennis balls were now made in Taiwan, India, and Australia. Slazenger still manufactured most of their tennis and squash rackets in London. Factory employees came mostly from inner London, many were recent East European or Indian immigrants and glad to have good jobs.

On the ground floor facing the street was their sales showroom. They had been producing rackets and balls for a hundred years and had several of their old rackets on display. Frank and I were invited to visit with their sales promotion manager, Bill O'Rourke, a portly, pink faced Irishman who knew the tennis and squash market like the back of his hand, welcomed us. He stubbed his cigarette, then got up and filled a paper cup with water, awaited the 'glug' from the large 3-gallon jug, an unpleasant sound that reminded him of his ulcer. He had been handling Frank's account for many years and had seen the expansion of his business firsthand. O'Rourke extended his hand to me in a warm respectful handshake saying, "I saw that punch on TV last summer", -"that was a beauty". He knew that I was coaching Michel and complimented me on his progress. I could see his gold cufflinks as he sat back down at his desk.

O'Rourke had no hesitation in asking Frank for his help in promoting Slazenger products. We were there to see the new version of their rackets and to help test the balls to be used at

Wimbledon. In return, Frank was always given free products and value discounts for his stores. O'Rourke told us that the company had just started a new automated ball factory in India to ensure a continuous supply of quality balls in the future. Because of cheap labor in India, this ensured stable low prices to preferred dealers like Frank. As usual Frank signed us up to do a few special promo clinics for kids in London, to play several exhibitions and attend 'meet and greet' parties for special clients and dealers.

As we were leaving O'Rourke gave me six of the new model rackets for Michel and me to use saying, "we appreciate your support". We took the old lift up to the top floor to meet the Managing Director in his office. The old historic lift smelled of stale leather, varnish, and paint as it creaked slowly upwards. We entered the manager's office, a large room with a high ceiling, distinguished mahogany desk and furniture, Persian rugs, and a breathtaking view of the Thames from an oversized bay window. We were escorted in by a very hot, young secretary wearing a light cream miniskirt with a matching cashmere sweater, minimal jewelry, and makeup. Just enough to set off her flawless, pale complexion. As she showed us in she looked right at me with her big blue eyes, and I whispered to her, "Looks like you need a tropical island holiday". She pursed her pink lips and nodded: "Yes. Yes!" I could feel my pulse quicken and my palms go damp.

Just then, the manager came in escorting two Pakistani men. One was the father of an international squash player, the legendary Hashim Khan. He was now over 50 and could still hold his own on the new professional squash tour. His son, a tall, lanky athlete in his 20's was currently #1 in the world. They were there for photos with their new signature model rackets. They were given several large boxes of the new model rackets and gut strings. They would take these back to Pakistan, avoiding all taxes and customs duty as these were classed as personal items. This was a common practice amongst all of us Australians, when we left the country Slazenger always gave us lots of rackets and gut string which we could sell in the countries we visited. The hot item overseas was the genuine sheep gut which was much in demand and sold for good prices at European tournaments.

Since our schedule had been altered by the rain, I found myself alone for dinner. My tastes frequently run toward Indian cuisine, which is not generally shared by Frank. I took this opportunity to visit an old Indian restaurant in East London. As I approached, I could smell the spices and Tandoori chicken in the air, bringing back memories with the anticipation of a great meal. A small, middle-aged man in a red turban showed me to a corner table at the back and handed me a well-worn menu that carried with it the aroma of Indian spices. He then bought nan bread and a large bottle of cold Indian beer and a chilled mug. It was early, but the dining room was already filling up, mostly with people immersed in quiet conversation, intent on listening to one another.

As I sat there and scanned the menu, my host went to the front of the crowded room and stood next to the two musicians who were providing quiet background music. With a nod to the waiter, the musicians started a new cadence. My waiter closed his eyes and began vocalizing to the strummed beat. As the music became more complex, he transitioned into a song in an Indian dialect that I did not understand. Despite the language barrier, I found the rhythm of the sitars almost intoxicating, blotting out all distractions and transporting me to a peaceful void in my mind. As is so often the case, a spontaneous dining choice turned into a delightful surprise. A waitress gently coaxed me from my trance to take my order.

The host stepped away from the music to continue his duties just as a waitress brought me a plate of curried lamb with Basmati rice. I sat there enjoying my meal with the beer and listened to the now very complex and lively instrumentals. In the middle of my meal, a rather scruffy looking man came in and sat next to me. He was unshaven, shabbily dressed and reeked of garlic. He looked like a dock worker or day laborer. His hands were clean but deeply calloused. I didn't have time to object to this as he occupied the seat so quickly. As I turned to question him, he muttered something in Indian. When I didn't respond and shook my head in confusion, he then leaned over and whispered in broken English into my ear, "Do you like the music?" Then he said, "What do you know about the Russian spy?"

I was taken aback and stared at him in confusion. "Wha..?" I started to say, but he just offered a crooked smile, placed his forefinger to his lips, and slipped out of his chair towards the door. I was left sitting there, mid-sentence, not knowing what he had been alluding to, or what my next move should be. I nervously looked around, and no one else seemed to have taken any notice of the man or our conversation. I shook my head to regain my composure and focused on my food in silence, without eating. After a moment or two I began to conclude that he had me mistaken for someone else and that his cryptic question had nothing to do with me. After all, I had no knowledge of or connection to any Russian spies. The sounds of the music were slowly drifting back into my head and chasing away any thoughts or concerns of spies.

The next morning, when we got to our court at Queens, Michel had already completed his running, stretching warmup routine and was about to start his serving practice. Frank and I got changed and joined him on the grass. My message to Michel for that day was "you need to play tennis as easily as you walk, run, or ride a bicycle. Once you have mastered playing automatically the next step is to learn to play with a quiet mind. It takes a quiet mind to play well under pressure. 'Learn to balance mind and body with experience. In our practices we need to work on your technique towards ultimate proficiency for you so as you can perform under pressure. Discover the technique that is naturally good for you. Don't try to copy what others may do." I advocate that aspiring tennis players learn their own natural swing early, preferably before age 12 including all the specialty shots such as drop shots, lobs, all the spins and so on and when to use them, and then practice all of them every day. "We have a lot of catching up to do over the next few weeks."

After some two on one drills for an hour we had a doubles match scheduled with the Knight brothers, the British #1 doubles team who I had played last year at Wimbledon. We were just starting the second set when Ludmilla showed up out of nowhere. She had on a very attractive short skirt which showed off her long legs. She appeared to have rich taste in jewelry. Her hair was pulled back and the emeralds that were dangling from her ears matched the sparkle of her deep green eyes and it was difficult to tell where her long blonde hair began and the gold around her neck started. Frank looked my way, expecting me to know what she was doing there. I shrugged. I had no idea. I had never said more than a few words to her at the party earlier in the week.

She stayed and watched. She was waiting for me when I left the locker room and latched onto my arm as I went out the main gate. She was a beautiful woman, obviously interested in me and difficult to resist. Her demeanor was shy and aggressive at the same time. I don't know how else to describe it. Her expression almost looked like that of an unsure schoolgirl, but her actions were sending signals that were loud and clear. She was looking into my eyes, seeking some kind of response.

5

Life Can Be Complicated

We stayed for a few drinks with very little conversation. She had taken the art of body language to a who new level, needing absolutely no translation and leaving no room for doubt as to her intentions, which had most of the men in the club wishing they were me. Somewhere between her bare foot scribing a line from my shoe to my inner thigh and her tongue flicking along the rim of her glass, I paid the tab, and we left the Queen's club in the descending twilight. I was feeling oddly uncomfortable with the situation. I could not deny that I was aroused by her mysterious appearance and the many glimpses of her flawless skin she had casually offered as we sat at the bar. Now her skin seemed to shimmer in the streetlights with each movement accentuating the well-toned muscles beneath it. We paused on the pavement and waited for two bicycles to pass. She gripped my hand tightly, hesitating just a little, as if searching for the correct words. "It was good to see you play tennis. You really are quite good. And very athletic" she said softly as if unsure of her English. A feeble "Thank you." was all I could manage. She paused again and seemed to be taking a deep breath to strengthen her resolve and confidence, finally blurting out "Your place or mine? You decide." Without giving me a chance to answer she hailed a taxi and gave the driver her address. It was a short, almost silent, ride. We got out and I paid the cabbie. She took my arm and ushered me up to her loft flat. I closed the door behind me keeping an eye on her sinuous moves, barely able to breathe with anticipation, as she turned and pushed herself against me, nimbly removing my belt. She leaned close to my neck and whispered in my ear that she "needs to f--k my brains out", no preliminaries, no drinks, no foreplay, just plain animal sex. She said she "needed me badly". I have seen other women respond similarly to the adrenaline-enhanced animal instinct that arises once they watch men play tennis! She spun us both around and backed me to the end of the couch, knocking me over backwards. She was on top of me pushing my shirt off my shoulders and removing my pants with such aggression and urgency as I had never seen before. It was contagious. Her total inhibition stripped me of any sense of tenderness and our actions were animal in nature. We rolled from the couch onto the shag rug. Her orgasm came on quickly with loud gasps and shrieks. At least I didn't have to hold off. Before I had even caught my breath, she was on me again, teasing, coercing, and building my desire, offering different positions as our bodies entangled and we moved over every available square inch of that rug, bumping into furniture and knocking over lamps. I almost felt as though I had been drugged, it was all so surreal. It was as if I had forgotten who I was. I must say that the whole evening was almost like a movie in which I was the lead male. Not exactly a feeling I would want to repeat. I couldn't quite put my finger on it; I somehow felt… used. We had coffee and vodka afterwards and I said I needed to go, "early day tomorrow practicing". As I reached for the door to leave, I turned and said, as gently as I could, that seeing her was an experience I would never forget, but my heart belonged to another woman. I didn't think we should pursue this relationship further. Listening to myself, I sounded like a cad, and I half expected an outburst of tears. Instead, she assured me that there was no need to worry. We were just consenting adults for the evening. Once again, that feeling of being used.

When I returned to Frank's, he told me more about her. He said she was about thirty, worked at the Russian embassy, and had a young daughter attending school outside of London. She also had a bit of a 'reputation' around men. I had met my first, and hopefully last, true nymphomaniac. He cautioned me to be careful as most people think that everyone working at the embassy is a spy. Her meeting me may or may not have been a coincidence.

We practiced again, the next day at Queen's. This time Yuri showed up to watch. He had a new bodyguard with him. They sat on the side bleachers. This was unusual as Yuri hadn't ever been to a practice before. He stayed and watched until we were done and then joined us for drinks afterwards. He insisted on paying the bill for all the drinks and lunch. He was obviously very pleased with how Michel was doing. He said privately to me how Michael's attitude appeared very professional and dedicated to his task. He thanked me for that.

When I had a moment alone with Yuri, I made a point of asking him about the torture and brutal murder of tennis player Roger Randall. He said he would check with his contacts who would probably know more about it. He said he would get back to me in a couple of days. If anyone could find out, Yuri could.

Frank apparently knew a guy who knew a guy and had arranged a meeting at a pub off Oxford Street. He was a bit disheveled and spoke in whispers with a Sicilian accent. While we were there, he was eyeballing the front door, appeared nervous, almost agitated. He was about fifty, wore one of those old Scottish caps that caddies in Scotland used to wear. He nervously fumbled with his butane lighter and lit up a cigarette, gave off a deep puff. Frank broke the stiff silence "You have something to tell us". Frank held up a twenty-pound note between two fingers looking the guy in the eye. There was a pause. The only sound was the clink of ice in his empty glass. He whispered in Frank's left ear "It was a sex ring. Roger was set up, paid the price of talking too much".

We needed to pass this information on to O'Neill. We tried to reach him by phone, only to remember that it was Saturday evening, and he wouldn't get the message until Monday. Frank and I decided to stop by his office in the morning and try to have someone reach him.

After a late supper with Frank at his house, I decided to take a walk. It was a cool but humid London evening and I needed to stretch my legs a bit. I was actually a bit sore and bruised after last night's rowdiness. After walking for an hour, I finished up at Susan's flat. I knocked on the door even though I still had the key she had given me. It was after midnight, but I knew she always worked 'til late. She was dressed in a short white silk summer robe and looked great to me. Before I had a chance to open my mouth, she had her arms wrapped around my neck, kissing me. She was so pleased to see me saying, "Don't talk, just keep kissing me". We spent the next two hours between small talk and making love.

Despite the late hour, a motorcycle passed by as I stepped out from her door. I watched as it continued to the next intersection, then turned left. The street was totally deserted except for a scrawny cat jumping down into the shadows from a trash container. I would need to walk a few blocks to find a cab at this time of night. As I approached an alley, I thought I saw movement, but the shadows were too deep, and I could see and hear nothing as I passed by. I quickened my step, feeling very nervous about being out alone this time of night on a dark street. In retrospect, not one of my better ideas. My heart was already racing from adrenaline when I felt a small pistol jabbed into my right rib cage. I could smell the man's breath as he grabbed my right arm and leaned closer to my ear. "Mr. Hardigan, you need to stop asking questions about the Roger Randall murder." He presses the gun a bit harder, and as he asks, "Do you understand?" I turned my head a bit to the right as if to answer, then using my well-trained core muscles, I whipped the rest of my body around, bringing my knee up suddenly to his groin, pulling my arm from his grasp. I brought my left hand up under his right arm and out, knocking the gun from his hand. I dove down and grabbed the pistol as he doubled over in pain. I accidentally caught the trigger and a shot cracked out. rolled back towards him, slamming the hot barrel into his head which was still within reach. He fell to the ground against a low fence, and I seized the moment to run, and run I did, as fast as I could, keeping the gun in full view. In the eerie half-light of the streetlamps, it seemed the world was in slow motion, and I was quicker than everyone else.

I made it to the end of the block, without looking back, almost running into a cab slowly cruising towards the intersection. I jerked open the door and yelled "Drive! Now!" as I pulled the door closed. I was able to see the gunman just starting to run after me, still limping in pain, as we pulled through the intersection. The Cabbie had broken into a sweat. I wasn't sure if he was afraid of getting shot at by whoever was chasing me, or if he was afraid of the lunatic with a gun that just jumped into his cab. I apologized about the gun and stashed it in my pocket. He visibly calmed down and asked if I was OK. I nodded and managed a "Yeah" in a shaky voice. I gave him Frank's address and put my head back against the seat, eyes closed, trying to stop shaking. I woke Frank, I was so revved up. I showed him the gun and the bruise on my rib cage. We stashed the gun in a plastic bag and put it in the safe, I got a well-deserved lecture about being stupid, while he handed me a shot of whiskey. I downed the shot and collapsed onto my bed. We would have lots to discuss at Scotland Yard in the morning. Maybe O'Neill could find some prints on the gun?

The next morning, we drove over to Scotland Yard. The officer on duty recognized us as civilians working with O'Neill on occasion. We explained that it was imperative that we speak to O'Neill, that it was in regard to the Roger Randall murder. He pointed out that it was Sunday morning, and the Lieutenant was most likely attending Mass. He asked us to have a seat and motioned to a line of old, well worn, wood armchairs with no cushions and very uncomfortable slatted straight backs. By the time he came over to us, my butt was sore and my back tight. He was able to track down the Lieutenant and he said his response was "This better be worth it!" He would be there in about 30 minutes. We got up to walk around the block to get the blood flowing in our legs again and by the time we returned, O'Neill was in his office, waiting.

I dropped the gun on his desk. It made a load thud in the quiet office. He glanced down at the gun, then up at Frank, then me. "You've been busy." was his only comment. He sat back in his chair, crossing his arms, and looked straight at me, patiently waiting for me to begin the tale he knew was coming. I described what happened last night and we relayed the minimal information from the man in the pub and the additional details provided by Yuri. He made a report on the attack and put the gun in for fingerprint and ballistic testing. We tediously went through his files of thugs who are known for these attacks. He thanked us and said, "be extra careful from now on". He then went over to his liquor cabinet, asked if we wanted a drink. Frank took one, I said, "it was too early for me". O'Neill slugged down a large swallow of his Irish whiskey, then stood gazing at the ice cubes in the bottom of his glass. It was as if he was looking into a crystal ball. His hand was very white, almost opaque, and mottled. As he downed his second slug, I noticed his hand trembling just slightly.

After leaving Scotland Yard, Frank decided to take the scenic route back to his house. It was early on a Sunday, and not many tourists around, so he chose to drive around Trafalgar Square and by Buckingham Palace to "see if the Queen was awake yet". The upper floors were lit up, and I could make out the guards at attention in their red coats by their pillboxes next to the main entrance. The gold paint glistened on the main gates in the morning sunlight. We drove around by Churchill's statue and the old Royal Navy Building just "to give me a feeling of proper reverence for the British Empire" now that I was back in Britain. According to Frank, " I was descendant of British genes and hailed from the Aussie antipodes". I decided to stay the night it would give me the opportunity to practice the next day before catching a late afternoon train back to Winston Gardens.

I took Frank to the embassy party. He always likes an opportunity to network and expand his global reach. The 'social hour' was more than a cocktail party. It was a meeting of the world diplomats. As usual, too eligible bachelors entering the room caught the eye of the female guests. Most of them, interested only in adding a character to their fantasies, would acknowledge us with a downward glance and hint of a smile, as they went back to whatever conversation they were involved in. As we were, in turn, scoping out the ladies in the room, we both spotted one woman in particular who seemed to be singularly focused on our arrival. I looked at Frank, because I could have sworn I heard a small gasp and sudden inhale coming from him. He was definitely staring in her direction, as she began to glide in our direction. It appeared we were about to meet the young and lovely Lucy, a beautiful Canadian attaché. She gave me the impression of a woman on a mission. Everything from her perfectly styled hair down to her Prada shoes spoke of confidence. As she got closer her face blossomed into a radiant smile, which was both warm and genuine. Not a very common site at these gatherings of politicians and brown-nosers. Despite her potentially elitist appearance, she was actually quite friendly and down to earth as she reached her hand out to me and allowed me to kiss it lightly. "Hi, I'm Lucy. You're that Aussie tennis player aren't you?" She smiled sweetly, cocking her head to one side and then, without waiting for an answer turned her full attention toward Frank. He took her extended hand and gazed into her eyes. All was lost. He was frozen in time, and she had to clear her throat to get him to snap out of his trance enough to release her hand. She didn't appear to mind at all, as a matter of fact, she seemed absolutely pleased with his reaction. She began chatting with us as if the three of us had been long lost mates. She fit into our conversation as easily as slipping on a comfortable shoe. Never having seen him like this before, I found Frank's uncharacteristic enchantment with her both somewhat humorous and yet heartwarming. He snapped out his stupor long enough to offer to get her a drink. That simple act seemed to bring him back to his normal smooth and suave self.

She batted her big blue eyes at him, and almost cooed when he took her hand to pass her the drink. She seemed a bit young for Frank but acted mature and confident and definitely came with all the right equipment. She made a point of telling us, and by us I mean Frank, that she was 'available' and that she would "do anything for us". The conversation was becoming more and more between them, including me only to be polite, so I excused myself and left them alone while I did a meet and greet around the room. Frank spent the evening plying her with Australian champaign and the two of them left together, I presume heading to his place. Overall, it was a pleasant evening, during which I had the opportunity to discuss the latest Australian wines with some diplomat that was particularly fond of the many varieties available from the southern coastal areas. Our host had joined us at one point and added his knowledge of the subject. Other conversations included my favorite subject, Wimbledon.

I left Frank to his own devices and went over to Susan's for a late supper. I took her a bottle of the Australian wine which she loved. I got at her flat about an hour before she got there, let myself in with my key and made us a light supper of Ham, cheese, salad and good crusty bread from the bakery downstairs. She was pleased, as always, to see me. I had been struggling a bit, after several conversations on the subject with Frank, about whether I should continue seeing Susan. After my own experience of 'feeling used' I wondered if I was no better than Ludmilla. I know Susan and I had a no strings attached arrangement, but now I was questioning if that was in any way fair to Susan. We talked long into the night. She had matured and come into her own, being more self-reliant, more confident. When I left her flat, I left the key behind.

"Smooth, toned hips and buttocks, breasts that were firm and stood on their own, yet soft and comfortable, and those gorgeous big blue eyes..." was how Frank would describe Lucy to me in the morning. He was definitely smitten. He, Michel, and I practiced again at Queen's as he got me up to speed about his new girl. He spent the night with her and said that they could become an item. It was the first time I heard Frank make that statement.

I caught the afternoon train to Winston Gardens carrying several great South Australian wines for Mirium, courtesy of our host at the ambassy, who remembered her from previous parties, and six new Slazenger rackets for me.

Mirium was very glad to see me. We had a nice quiet evening together, catching up over a light dinner of pasta and chicken. We retired to the bedroom and lounged on the bed as we talked about how Roger had been so brutally murdered, recalling Dom's untimely death by the assassin at Wimbledon's main gate last year and my close calls with the murder on Oliver Street and with the Irish Terrorist group. Recalling the graphic photos of Roger's tortured corpse, I found my mind wandering to stories my father used to tell of the gory torture of Australian prisoners by the Japanese in World War II.

We must have dozed off as I found myself transported into a dream. I was my father, the coast watcher, in the jungles of New Guinea.

Feeling a little better today. Still some lingering effects of dysentery and malaria in my system, running a fever, sore throat, no energy. Just need to get to some place dry - away from the bugs, mold, and constant wetness. No air drop of food this month - Japs are watching for it.

The truck stopped on the muddy track - the 'rising sun' on the side. Four Japs stepped out to take a piss. From my position in the dense jungle at the side of the road I could see the sweat on their shirts. When they leaned against the truck to take a smoke in the shade, I could smell the cheap tobacco. Should I take them out or stay hidden?

Best to keep quiet; let them move on - I need to keep silent, stay alive! I was due to send my next message out that night after dark - then move on to stay undetected.

My faithful native 'fuzzy wuzzie' guide, Kendo, wanted to take them out. He hated the Japs - called them 'septics'. However, to do that would bring the whole Japanese army down on us. We knew only too well that we were well behind enemy lines, Do nothing stupid. Don't leave any tracks. Keep it quiet. Just change positions every day and send off radio reports on shipping, as undetected as possible.

It appeared from my last two coastal channel observations that Japanese shipping lanes were filling up with more troop transports and minesweepers. Two more of the big destroyers today. Thankfully, no coastal patrols. Best to keep quiet and move to the next headland for a better view, undetected.

During this time the Japanese were invading New Guinea and threatening Australia with invasion. They had already taken the Solomon Islands and had 30,000 men ready to land on the east peninsula - unprotected except for an out-manned Australian garrison. The jungle there was mosquito infested, swampy, and mountainous towards Port Moresby. Most of the Australians got swamp or glandular fever and chances of malaria were high. With the help of the Papua natives and a few Americans, we Aussies held.

As Kendo and I turned to disappear into the jungle, a Japanese squadron was approaching. They spotted us, and before we could retreat in another direction, they had surrounded us. We were taken prisoners and restrained on nearby trees.

I was suddenly pulled out of my fitful sleep, as Mirium was violently shaking me, and calling my name to wake me. I was drenched in sweat. She had awakened me just as our captures were approaching in the dream, with weapons of various sorts to use to torture us, just as Roger had been strung up, defenseless and tortured. I lay there, in Mirium/s arms, as she wiped the sweat from my brow. It had all been so very real, so very, very real! Like I was there. Maybe this was a warning…

6

Commitment

Courtesy of the Australian Tennis Federation, I got one of their wild cards straight into Wimbledon Qualifying without having to play at Frinton or Bournemouth, which suited me just fine. I could spend the next few weeks training Michel and getting him ready for Junior Wimbledon. I was hopeful we would qualify for Gentleman's Doubles by virtue of a wild card. When Wimbledon started, Michel would be the number four ranked British junior. Playing doubles together would be a great experience for both of us and give us a great goal to work on together. I was very proud of his progress so far with his technique, overall attitude, and professionalism. He had even learned how to handle the vociferous British press. There were always questions about his tics to his uncle, as a known London underworld figure. There was a picture of Michel and I in the sports section of the Telegraph, 'Practicing at Queens'. It was part of a feature on British hopes for Wimbledon coming up. The article was particularly kind to Michel, probably due to his uncle Yuri's influence. It also mentioned again that I was the 'Wimbledon Killer Catcher' from last year, so as Frank says everyone knows me as the killer catcher. He said that Slazenger loved the free extra publicity and had already signed me up to do a few pre-Wimbledon exhibitions. Right next to the picture in the paper they had a half page ad for Slazenger Balls, "Wimbledon's choice for over fifty years".

The next embassy party was outside on the back terrace of the embassy as it was a nice warm afternoon. As Frank and I arrived we were directed around the building towards the cackle of human voices in the rear. It appeared to us like a chicken farm with all the chickens cackling at the same time. There were many foreign accents and languages, with most people talking without bothering to do any listening. What a din! As we moved up onto the terrace, we were checked in by a very courteous Australian soldier in full kaki uniform with traditional Aussie slouch hat, buttoned down on one side. By the sound of things, the party was in full swing with much good Australian beer and wine flowing freely. As we got our first drinks, out of nowhere a very robust middle-aged woman blustered to me "out here", directing us to the back of the crowd. Frank whispered to me "we'd best follow her" and as we followed "this is the richest woman in London". We followed. By now she had a vice grip on my left arm. I took a quick look to my left as we skirted around through a bunch of inebriated guests. As she dragged me through the crowd, I tried to estimate, in dollars, just how much this woman was worth.

She took me straight over to meet the ambassador, who remembered me from past parties. He was a pasty white bald type with a pronounced paunch, probably from eating and drinking too much on his expense account. After meeting the dignitaries, Carol, I think her name was, turned to me and said, 'Jack, you need to meet my daughter Heidi.' She then proceeded to drag me around the terrace to meet her daughter. The daughter's eyes appeared a little glazed, maybe a bit drunk. She looked right past me as though I wasn't there. Carol introduced us saying, "Heidi, this is Jack Hardigan, you remember the boy we watched play on centre court last year, the one who was in all the papers, the hero who cornered the killer in the stands, right next to the Royal Box?".

Heidi suddenly warmed up to me, thrusting her hand under my right elbow so I had Carol on one arm, and Heidi on the other. Just then a waiter appeared with glasses of the new South Australian champaign which gave me an excuse to release Carol's iron grip. Heidi, in turn took a glass and released her grip, only to place her hand down on my buttock. She obviously was interested in men. The daughter had this, elegant angular look about her though was a bit thin for my taste. After her mother's invitation she certainly had latched onto me, and as it appeared to me, would not be letting go soon. I was stuck. We sat down on a low wall, watching the sun set. All I can remember is the smell of her Chanel perfume and that she was talking about herself and all her problems, nonstop. She was one of those very self-absorbed types, making it hard to have a mutual conversation.

While I was fending off Heidi, Frank came over and saved me. He had his Canadian girlfriend on his arm, instantly saw I needed relief and just swept me away. We had one more drink, then decided to go for dinner before we got too smashed. I really liked Lucy and thought she was a good match for Frank. I was to go back to Winston Gardens in the morning, so I invited Frank and Lucy up for the weekend. I wanted Mirium to meet Lucy, Frank and I could practice on Mirium's grass courts, we could ride the horses, and spend time by the pool. It would be a good break for Lucy to get away from her work at the embassy. I called Mirium that evening. She was delighted and would meet me at the station in the morning. We all looked forward to a great weekend.

Mirium met me in her maroon Jaguar XJ6 at the station. We had a good day at the estate, took a long walk through the countryside, enjoying the comfortably warm afternoon. Her local chef came in and fixed us a very simple pasta dish followed by local venison with roasted potatoes. We sat and chatted on the back veranda and watched a beautiful sunset. Everyone was lulled into the relaxed country vibe of the day, and we all retired early. This is how life should be!

The next morning, I woke early to the sound of mowers on Mirium's grass courts. Mirium looked like an angel, peacefully asleep, her face lit by a shaft of light that managed to sneak in through a small gap between the draperies, as if it was determined to find her at that very moment. Her hair was tossed over the edge of the pillow, her skin looked as smooth as silk. I put on my shorts and decided to take a run. As I passed by the kitchen, I could smell bacon and eggs cooking and told the cook I would be back in about half an hour. It was one of those misty, foggy mornings, quite cool for summer, but invigorating as I ran. As I hit the dirt road out of the estate, I noticed two men parked in a dark sedan. When they saw me heading towards them they drove off. I didn't recognize the car. I thought to myself that Mirium may need to rehire her security firm, especially after O'Neill's warning. Besides, Mirium had many valuable paintings and a safe full of valuables.

When I returned for breakfast, Mirium was up. I told her about the dark car on the road out front. She immediately called her security firm and had them send over someone. He then spent the morning upgrading the security cameras and alarm system. We both felt the upgrade was needed, especially since we had travel plans coming up. She usually had her head gardener and his wife stay in the old coach house when she went out of town.

We spent the morning in the shade by the pool, then a light lunch. It was nice to laze around with Mirium. She was always good company. By the pool the air was fresh with a faint scent of the pines nearby. The sky was clear and blue with very few clouds. I lowered my legs to the side of the chaise lounge so I could soak up the lines of her body in her white, one piece backless, bathing suit. I wished, at that moment, I could paint her in oils for posterity. This is about as good as it gets. Once again I felt I was a very lucky man to be here at this moment in time.

Michel showed up around 2pm for our workout. Yuri had given him a new MGB which made his commute easier, not to mention, very enjoyable for him. We had a good, tough training session which tired me out. Michel and I returned from the courts to poolside, glistening in perspiration. Mirium was there by the pool, looking magnificent as usual. She poured water from a crystal pitcher into two glasses and handed one to me and one to Michel, "Good practice?" she asked. Michel gave her a silent nod in agreement as he quickly took a drink of the water. She refilled his glass, and we sat down at a poolside table to sip our cool water. Michel was making progress with his game, a lot of it developmental as he is growing into his more mature body. He's a magnificent athlete, but his game still needs consistency and a lot of fine tuning. After a time to cool down and change into clean clothes, he headed off in his new car, back to London and confirmed that he'll be back Saturday, when Frank will be joining us. I then took a quick nap by the pool before tea. Frank had called while I was on the court and confirmed that he and Lucy would drive in tomorrow afternoon for the weekend. He said he had no news to report about the murder.

I told Frank about the suspicious black car outside our gates. We also talked on the phone about the brutal Milan murder of one of our British tennis players and went through our thoughts on motive and possible list of suspects. No news yet from O'Neill on this or identifying any prints on the gun. We understood that if the killers find out that we know something, we all may be in danger. As Frank said, "putting on extra security was very much a needed priority right now".

That evening we took a long drive in the country in the jaguar to one of our favorite country pubs. It was a popular watering hole for the locals with a great outdoor beer garden and excellent food. It was one of our preferred destinations. We had an excellent dinner with lots of conversation about our experiences together and future plans for travel. Mirium was obviously worried about O'Neill's dire warning but said she felt much safer when I was there with her.

As we were driving back, I noticed Mirium was very quiet. As we came near the front gate of her estate, she had started to say something, but stopped to comment on the lorry we had come up upon, that was slowly navigating the country road. I could tell she had something on her mind, a distraction of some kind. We stopped in the driveway, and she sat quietly still for a bit, then she said, "These past few days, having you back, have been wonderful", then her voice trailed off. She turned to me as tears began forming in her eyes and said softly "I like what we have.

I'm glad we found each other. We need to talk about our future together, Jack. I do love you and need you with me".

I was speechless for a moment. The world suddenly tilted, then righted itself. I took a deep breath then, breathed out slowly, just as I do in my tennis matches. Mirium pressed her lips together as the tears gathered. Here I was sitting in the moonlight with this beautiful, intelligent woman, almost in tears. At that moment, for the only the second time since we had met, she seemed totally vulnerable. The first was when she quietly entered my bed for the first time. It seemed like a lifetime ago yet was just last summer. This moment was so important, and my next words would mold my entire future. I needed time to think how to respond. I slowly placed my right hand on hers and leaned toward her to reach across with my left hand to tenderly touch her chin, gently turning her head to look towards me. She finally lifted her gaze up to my face, as I began to speak. "I thought you were happy keeping things the way they are". But, yes, I love you very much and want to be with you, too." Her face started to brighten a bit. Then I said, "We've talked about me starting my postdoctoral work at Oxford in the fall. I do want to make something of myself, to make a contribution to the world and be someone deserving of you. I want to be someone we can both be proud of." "Oh, Jack" she started to say, and I placed my finger on her lips so I could continue. "I also want nothing more than to have you in my life along that journey."

She grasped both of my hands; her tears were gone. "Is this a proposal Jack?" I responded as a broad smile came across my face and I gazed directly into her eyes "I guess it is". "I've known we are a great team, but I wasn't sure how you felt about this until now. I was trying to figure out how to do this for quite a while". We punctuated the conversation with a long, tender kiss there in the moonlight then went inside, arm in arm. As Mirium opened some champagne, and I told her I'd be right back, I ran upstairs. I came back down, and she had two glasses in her hand. I carefully took them from her and put them down on the bar. She looked at me questioningly as I reached into my pocket and took out a small box. Her hands went to her mouth as she let out a small gasp. I slowly lowered onto one knee before her and opened the box to reveal my mother's diamond ring, which I had been carrying around with me for just this moment. "Mirium, would do me the honor of becoming my wife?" The tears began to flow freely, this time from joy, as she barely managed to speak the word I wanted to hear. "Yes." My mother would have loved Mirium. "Think of this ring as a symbol to seal our plans for our future together". Though it was a modest ring, Mirium seemed to genuinely love it. Beside the euphoric glow about her, she seemed as if every bit of tension and stress had gone from her face and indeed from her whole body. She admitted that she was always afraid that I would grow tired of her and leave. I should have told her how I felt sooner.

Later, I went upstairs to take a shower. I started thinking about this day. This was very much a turning point in my life. Perhaps 'only once in his life, a man has his time, this was my time'. A great philosopher once said, "some people improve life by just existing". Mirium was one of those people. "The secret of life is to like what you do and to share some of it with someone you love".

Right there, my life had changed in an instant. I believe we all live parallel lives when we try to answer, "What if." It appeared now my life had permanently changed. From now on, there were to be no more multiple women. I had too much to lose. It was time to settle down and cherish what I had in this lifeline. It was all about choice, and I was committed to this path. In a parallel life I would have gone on doing just what I had been doing and would have missed the greatest adventure in life.

She went to the mirror, took a tissue, and blotted her bright red lipstick. I watched her looking at herself. Her face showed no tension. She smiled at me in the mirror, and our eyes met. It was as though we were looking at ourselves for the first time.

7

Lausanne

Mirium had received a letter that day from her Swiss banker in Lausanne. In the letter, along with her usual financial statements, was inventory of her deceased husband's fine art collection. She had originally thought we could take a trip to view the collection after Wimbledon, but it seemed that the bank was planning on moving the collection to a new facility and it was necessary for her to verify the collection before they could plan the move. She expressed her desire to fly down there in the next few days to. She admitted to me, "This list tells me that there is a lot more of value that I imagined". She hoped that my schedule would allow me to accompany her for a few days in Switzerland. Based on the inventory that they had provided, the potential that some of the pieces, which were already quite valuable, may have significantly increased in value over the years, most likely requiring an adjustment to the insurance coverage.

The next morning, I checked my schedule for the coming week, and I had nothing planned until Wednesday. Mirium called and scheduled a meeting for Monday afternoon and had arrangements made for our flight and hotel. Part of me still wasn't quite used to the idea of just hopping on a plane for a 'daytrip', especially not one to Switzerland. I found the thought of it oddly humbling, as I recalled my early life in Australia in contrast to the life I had ahead of me. I hoped that I would never forget those humble beginnings.

Frank showed up with Lucy as promised. Lucy, being accustomed to paying attention to details, noticed the ring on

Mirium's lefthand within 5 minutes of arriving and had let out a shriek and a "You're engaged!" Frank nearly lost his footing, he turned to look at Mirium's hand so quickly then spun back to look at me. I have to admit, I have never seen him be this surprised by anything. His initial verbal reaction he caught short in deference to the ladies present. As Lucy and Mirium giggled and chatted, he quietly said something to the effect of, "You sneaky son of a b..tch! Why didn't you tell me?" I explained that it was rather spontaneous and just happened last night. After the fuss over our engagement and some more formal introductions, the remainder of the weekend proceeded as if we had all been best friends and couples for years. Lucy and Mirium got along famously. Lucy was charming. Conversation came easily to her, and she was eager to listen and learn about her newfound friends. She was also very attentive to Frank through the entire weekend, without being overly doting, but obviously enjoying his company and not just the overall experience. Michel arrived after lunch on Saturday and was focused on his training. He seemed oblivious to all else around him. After Michel left to return to London, our weekend was spent in a relaxed and unhurried 'living-the-dream' manner, with horseback riding, lounging by the pool, sipping cocktails, great meals and even an evening at the local pub. We got Mirium and Lucy out on the courts for some just-for-fun tennis. It was actually more like a comedy routine, as Lucy had never played before, and we were all feeling quite relaxed from the cocktails by the pool. It was a marvelously normal weekend.

Lucy and Frank had commitments first thing Monday morning, so they headed back to the city on Sunday evening. We were exhausted from relaxing, if that made any sense, so we packed for our trip to Lausanne right after they left and made an early night of it.

The next morning was clear and warm. We awoke early, I went for a run then joined Mirium for a short swim. After breakfast by the pool and showers, we were off for Switzerland.

The flight from London to Lausanne was an hour and 30-minute, non-stop trip. There was a driver waiting at the gate, holding a sign for Mirium, who led us to the limo that would take us directly to the bank.

It was only a 15-minute drive to the banking district in Lausanne. The roads in that area were cobblestone, with tandem buses, scooters, cars, and pedestrians bustling around amongst the many stately buildings. To my untrained eye, it appeared that Greek architecture was a major influence in the building designs. Many of the buildings had seen upgrades to modern windows and doors. The entrances were massive. and the interiors, while updated, still had the feel and many of the features of the original structures, with marble floors and vaulted ceilings. The security for the main vault at the Lausanne Hauser Bank was impressive. Only thoroughly screened clients and accredited bank personnel could enter. At the present bank location, the art collections were in an underground, fireproof, secure basement. Access was only granted by special fingerprinted pads. The whole secured basement, the size of a football field was state of the art but was not big enough to accommodate present and future clients' collections.

When we entered the bank, Mirium was greeted by the head banker, who, after being properly introduced to me and allowed the time to do a quick background check to assure the bank that I was indeed who she said I was, escorted us to her holdings. While we waited, he mentioned that there was no need for her to have rushed down there, as they would not move the artwork for several weeks. She was very surprised at what was in her art closet. Of particular interest to her was an obscure Van Gogh, buried in the inventory. Van Gogh was very prolific and had painted many works which were undocumented. She believed this was one of those forgotten works. She took some photographs of it and left it there. Knowing that the bank was soon to move all their holdings to their newer, secured, climate-controlled vault and she knew that it was going to be necessary to get it appraised by a verified expert.

The next morning, at the banker's recommendation, we would take the photograph and original bill of sale to their preferred art expert for appraisal.

The bank manager had arranged for the limo to take us to our hotel near the shores of Lake Geneva, where we had already made a reservation. As the car passed under the sign marking the entrance to the hotel grounds, I noticed the words, "One of The Leading Hotels in the World". I was looking forward to our stay. The front desk staff greeted us warmly, as if they were sincerely pleased that we chose to stay at their establishment. As they handed us the keys to our suite, they mentioned that it was just two years ago that Bruce Willis stayed in that same room. They also mentioned their afternoon tea was from 2 – 6 in the Lobby Lounge. We went up to our room to freshen up and then spent some time walking along the lake, towards Olympic Park, enjoying the flowers on one side and the view of the Alps across the lake on the other. In the opposite direction we were able to browse through some of the local shops. We took advantage of the afternoon tea in the Lobby Lounge and enjoyed some light pastries with our tea. The ionic columns supporting the roof over the veranda enhanced the already beautiful view of Lake Geneva and added a romantic touch to the peaceful scene. I noted that ring on Mirium's hand and felt a swell of a mixture of pride of having the honor of calling her 'my fiancée' and love for this incredible woman sitting across from me. Her eyes met mine and a light flush crept into her cheeks.

The next morning, we took a cab to the recommended art expert. The bank had called and made an appointment, but since it was so last minute, and the appraiser had a couple of other meetings to attend to, he was going to have to squeeze us in as he could. After quite a bit of waiting, we finally got to meet him. When he walked into the waiting room, we hadn't expected that he was the gentleman we were waiting for. He was a bit scruffy looking, with an unkempt beard, wearing a well-worn, brown sports coat that looked like 'something the cat had dragged in'. He mumbled "I'll be with you in a moment." as he rushed past us through a door in the waiting room. The afternoon before, Mirium had made a call to her bank in London to have his credentials checked. Upon seeing him, she made another quick call to the bank here in Lausanne to verify his appearance. The manager here chuckled and said her concern was totally understandable, and he should have warned us about his appearance. It would have been very difficult to believe the man that just rushed through the waiting room was a highly respected art appraiser. His secretary came out and said he could see us now. We were ushered into a small, and cluttered, office with floor to ceiling shelves lining two walls, holding volumes of books in every area of art. There was what appeared to be a substantial vault on another wall. The room had the smell of old books, leather, and a faint aroma of old cigars, probably from an era gone by. It sounded as if there was an air filter of some sort running constantly while we were there, presumably to keep the air circulating to prevent the odors of the past from seeping into any client's art pieces that he might have in his possession. He took a pair of glasses out of his jacket pocket and scrutinized the documents the bank had supplied and the photograph thoroughly, his eyebrows occasionally rising, showing obvious, but controlled, excitement at this intriguing discovery. Apparently the bank had not mentioned the subject of our visit. He consulted several volumes that he had taken from the shelves in his office, placing them on top of the open books already strewn on his desk, and, then, taking his glasses off and looking at us with a glow of excitement, he very matter-of-factly, disclosed, that if this painting was a genuine original work, it was a heretofore unknown work of van Gogh and as such, it was now worth a minimum of 2.5 million US dollars! At auction, it would most likely demand a substantially higher price. It took a moment for our minds to process this statement. It was particularly difficult for me to wrap my head around numbers that large. I couldn't believe it! Mirium took it all in stride, as usual. She was used to dealing with large sums of money. But 2.5 million USD? Wow! He made it very clear that he could not give us a formal appraisal until he had actually seen the painting and had an independent verification of its authenticity. After a brief discussion regarding the importance of keeping the existence of this piece absolutely quiet, we told him we would be in touch to arrange for an official inspection of the original, stating that it would be a week or two before we got back to him. We had to coordinate with the bank and Wimbledon was coming up, which I would be competing at. We collected our paperwork, shook hands, and left his office.

We decided celebration was in order and we walked a few blocks to a small French restaurant for lunch. I commented that Lausanne was not one of the most picturesque cities in Switzerland, but it would be a convenient starting point for a train trip through the Alps.

We had already packed our luggage and left it at the front desk of the hotel. We caught a cab and stopped to pick it up on the way to the airport. We planned the rest of our week on the plane back to London. I had a meeting with Yuri the next day and then two clinics that I had agreed to do for Slazenger on Thursday. I also needed to practice as much as I could and keep Michel focused on his practices. Mirium had a meeting with her foundation board scheduled for Thursday and wanted to do some shopping in town, so we decided that she should stay in London with me. One of the things I loved about her was that she didn't depend on me to keep her busy. She was independent and self-sufficient and had enough interests to take up her days when I was busy. We were a very good match for each other.

We took the train to London the next day and went directly to Frank's. This was the first time Mirium had seen his place. As I had been the first time entering, she was very impressed with the security for the building. I gave her a quick tour of his flat and headed out to meet Yuri. She was going to relax a bit then head over to the Notting Hill Farmers' Market and Portobello Rd. market. She had decided that it was time for her to demonstrate her culinary abilities and she wanted to pick up some fresh ingredients. She would make dinner for Frank, Lucy, and I that evening.

I was to meet Yuri on Kensington High St., between Melbury and Hollandgreen. It was a pleasant walk, not too hot and not too humid. His smile broadened as I approached the car he was seated in. He invited me to join him in the car, and we would go "grab a bite to eat." The car was a large black Rolls Royce, and being invited to ride with him was an indication that this was a friendly liaison. There always appeared an intelligence in his eyes, as if he knew something you didn't. Despite his gangster reputation, since I had been coaching his young nephew, Michel, he had impressed me with his forthrightness and humility. Michel appeared to have many of his qualities, whether inherited or through interaction with him, I wasn't sure. Yuri always paid me well for the time spent with his nephew, praising my coaching as he witnessed the progress his nephew was making. He also, in many ways, was an honest man who conducted himself with integrity. Despite warnings from outsiders, I thought of Yuri as a loyal friend, supporter and confidante. He was glad to see me. Not a bad reaction, considering his status in the London underworld. He almost embarrassed me with how much he repeated how pleased he was with how his nephew, Michel, had progressed with his tennis. He was even more impressed at the maturing and development of his character. He emphasized, "This is very much your doing! Michel is fast becoming a man with maturity and attitudes far beyond his already exceptional physical achievements."

His chauffeur took us to an upscale Polish restaurant named Polska. We sat down and had perogies with a subtlety complex sauce and, of course, accompanied by only the finest Russian vodka. Even though it was lunchtime, I decided it was prudent to join in a toast, or two, to Michel's progress out of respect for Yuri. I had to keep in mind, that although our relationship was friendly, this was still a man you did not want to offend or cross. I had it on the rocks, which is the only way I can drink it without suffering a massive headache the next day.

As we got up to leave, he passed me another envelope, this time, as it turned out, with £5000 in it. I took it and shook his outstretched hand, unaware of the amount. "This is just a discreet 'Thank You' for all of your time."

8

The Russian Spy

I returned to Frank's to the heavenly aroma of Northern Italian cooking. Mirium was busy in the kitchen and seemed totally at home and in control. Apparently, one of her favorite pastimes when she traveled abroad, was to take a lesson in local cooking techniques. I hadn't realized that was 'a thing' but apparently many locales have these available for tourists, and if not, Mirium had no qualms about asking a local chef to indulge her with a private lesson. The bright colours of the fresh vegetables created an artist's palette against the ebony-coloured marble top of the centre island. She had a pan of cream sauce with mushrooms and spinach simmering on the stove top, ready to toss with fettuccine. A salad bowl filled with greens, red onions, roasted red peppers and cucumbers sat off to the side. She was just whisking together the ingredients for a creamy Tuscan dressing. The pan on the stove had clarified butter ready to cook the thick veal chops she had prepped for Veal Milanese. She had prep dishes with fresh rosemary sprigs, crushed fresh garlic, salt and pepper ready to use just the right amount of seasoning. As my gaze swept the room, I was once again reminded what an amazing woman I was to have as my wife.

Frank arrived moments after me, followed by Lucy about 30 minutes later. Not surprisingly, Mirium had selected a suite of wines to cover our libations for the evening and loosen our tongues for lighthearted conversation.

Just as we had finished our dinner, the phone rang, and Frank excused himself to answer it. In his business, he couldn't afford to not check to see who it was that was interrupting his evening. He looked at the caller ID and recognized the number as that of Inspector O'Neill. He picked up the phone and warily greeted the inspector, expecting that this was not a social call and likely did not mean good news. O'Neill responded, "Hello, Frank." then immediately asked for me. As I got up to take the call in the next room, I wondered how the inspector knew where to find me, He apologized for interrupting our supper hour, but he felt this was important. He said I might need to know that a corpse was dumped outside of Yuri Grosegann's nightclub that evening. It turns out that the man was an employee of the Russian Embassy, which could only mean one thing. He was a spy. O'Neill felt that since I was coaching Yuri's nephew, I was in a need-to-know position. There was no telling what the connection was that led to this man's death.

I returned to the after-dinner conversation, keeping the news to myself for the moment, to allow us all to enjoy our evening. I simply responded to the questioning looks with a smile and "The good inspector would like to see me again in the morning." I could tell by Mirium's look that she didn't believe that was all there was to the conversation. I gave her a wink and glanced at Lucy and Frank as they sat on the couch, thoroughly enjoying the wine and each other. We didn't want to disturb the mood of the evening.

I left to take Mirium to Waterloo station for the 9 pm train back to Winston Gardens. She understood that I had a lot of preparation for the qualifying matches and needed to concentrate on my game, as well as get Michel ready for his rounds. She graciously conceded that she would be too much of a distraction for me and it was best if she stayed at home. During the cab ride, I told her about the conversation with Inspector O'Neill and told her I would keep her informed as I found out more, assuring her that there was most likely no connection to us at all. As I got back into the cab after dropping her off I noticed someone leaning against a car up ahead of us, lighting a smoke. I guessed that he was just waiting for someone arriving at the station, but he made me feel uneasy, just the same. As my cab passed the parked car, the man got into the driver's seat. I called Mirium later to be sure she made it home without incident.

Love has a lot to do with timing. It's something that can just take you over, where that special person can take over all of your thoughts. As I prepared for my qualifying matches, I wasn't quite sure how this new commitment to Mirium would affect me. However, I was glad we had found each other and had some kind of long-term commitment. I was happy with this and was hopeful this would stabilize my life. I agreed with one of Mirium's favorite sayings, "many people work so hard at living, without really knowing how to live".

Frank had left early the next morning to catch up on some paperwork at the office. When I left the building, I noticed an unremarkable Volkswagen Passat sedan, with a somewhat unkempt looking chap standing alongside it looking straight at me, as if waiting for me. I remembered the car and driver I saw at the train station the night before. He called my name, startling me, and introduced himself as Michael Ladden, said he was sent by O'Neill. I hesitated to get into his vehicle, and with a hand gesture to indicate hold that thought, I quickly turned and went back into the lobby of the building. I went over to security and asked them to use their phone. I made a quick call to O'Neill, who surprisingly actually answered his phone quickly, to confirm the identity of this stranger. He apologized for not letting me know in advance, but he had been extra busy with security details for Wimbledon. O'Neill explained that he was a former MI5 officer assigned to me. While the murder of Roger had most likely been due to his own greed, that had not been confirmed yet, and in light of the previous threats to me, O'Neill felt it was prudent to keep me under surveillance. I returned to the curb where Ladden was patiently waiting for me, understanding now how the Inspector knew my whereabouts last evening. I quickly sized him up. He had almost black eyes, dark hair, probably dyed, square cheekbones, with badly pocked cheeks. He was very intense and a chain smoker, Pall Mall being his chosen smoke. According to

O'Neill, he could follow anyone, undetected in crowds or otherwise. He was to discreetly follow Mirium, and I whenever we were in London, such was O'Neill's concern for our safety. Mirium already had her own security surveillance at her estate.

Michael figured the easiest way to keep an eye on me was to drive me around when I was alone. The first stop this morning was Scotland Yard to learn the details about the information O'Neill had passed on to me the evening before.

Yesterday had been a foggy evening and it had been early when the body was dumped on the sidewalk right outside the main entrance to Yuri's club. The body was that of a man, fully clothed, in a grey suit. It was a tall, muscular man of about forty. It was clear this was a message as he had been garroted with the head almost severed from the body.

When a corpse appears just outside of Yuri's club, who just happens to be a 'Russian Embassy Employee', i.e., a Russian spy, it becomes a top priority and raises a lot of questions. It turned out that this particular body was easily identifiable, albeit by some blatant stereotyping, in his dark suit and long overcoat which was a bit heavy for this time of year, and the scar across his left cheek.

When Scotland Yard appeared at the scene, the body was mostly devoid of ornamentation, except for a pen clipped to the inside chest pocket of the overcoat. Close inspection of the pen revealed a microchip affixed to the barrel. The team back at the Yard was able to read the chip and immediately notified M15. The information on the chip was the complete plans for the upgrade to the London power grid, which would imply that a terrorist attack was being planned that would involve taking out the power to the something critical in the city, if not the entire city. Apparently, whoever murdered this individual was unaware of the importance of the pen and was not interested in anything the spy was involved in. The murder was apparently not related to the activities of the deceased but was just a statement meant for Yuri.

As we were leaving, I wanted to call Yuri and Michael suggested using the payphone in the lobby of the building rather than the one at the street corner. "Less likely an assassin would hit inside Scotland Yard" was his reasoning. I'm sure that statement was meant as assurance, but somehow it had the opposite effect. I hadn't thought of myself as a target before he put it that way. I called Yuri from inside the building.

Yuri admitted that he did know the man and asked that I tell him of anything that the police discovered about the incident. He also stressed that I should be vigilant and alert, especially when working with Michel, and especially concerning any strangers that I notice lurking around. I mentioned that someone had been assigned to keep an eye on Mirium and me whenever we were in London, and that she had recently updated her security at her home. He was glad to hear that.

From that point on, Yuri was sure to have a bodyguard in constant attendance wherever Michel and I were. He viewed this 'gift' as a warning from his opposition that the Russians could easily be taken down.

We picked Frank up at his office. Michael dropped us off at Frank's, and we walked to the corner pub so we could work out a practice schedule for the next few days. I noticed Michael had found a parking spot across from the entrance to the pub. This should have made me feel secure, but somehow it made me feel tense. We wrote down the schedule of the back of a napkin, and I handed it to Michael when we left the pub. Frank, Michel and I spent most of the next three days together, practicing any chance we could get at the Queen's courts, and if not there at any number of other grass practice courts throughout London. With all the contenders trying to get as much practice time in as possible, court time was at a real premium. Frank's status in the sports community carried some weight and made it a bit easier to get access to courts around the city. I was glad I had all of the court time I needed up to this point at Winston Gardens as well as the training sessions with Michel at Queen's earlier in the season. When we weren't on the courts, I was coaching Michel on the mental side of the game and trying to get myself in the proper frame of mind to focus. That was particularly difficult with Ladden shadowing me, a reminder that I could be in danger myself.

I awoke the morning of my qualifying match with a splitting headache. Michael was waiting at the curb, an eerie visage through the mist and gloom. Today was to be cloudy and overcast with low clouds. What else could it be, this was London, the week before Wimbledon. Thankfully, no rain was forecast for the afternoon when my match was scheduled. Frank joined me for a short warmup and a light lunch at Queens.

I was lucky enough to get a good draw in qualifying, won two close matches at the Hampton Road courts and got a default for the third match. Suddenly, I found myself heading to Centre Court, on National television. I was to be playing three-time Wimbledon champion Boris Becker. Becker, who won his first title as a very athletic teenager, was a national hero in Germany, losing to another German, Michael Stich, just last year. Boris's ability to stay focused on his game was unnerving, and he was a true master on the grass,

I knew I had the skills to beat him, but my mental game was indeed going to be a challenge.

9

A Swim in the River

Back at Frank's place, I took a long soak in his hot tub and sipped one of the many fine brandies he had available. I gave Mirium a call and spent an hour on the phone with her. I hadn't realized how much I missed having her near until I heard her voice. There was a lot of catching up to do and once that was over, the sexual innuendos began creeping into the conversation and I missed her even more.

Frank came home to find me asleep on the couch with the TV on. I woke up when he clicked the off button on the remote. This was the first opportunity for Frank and me to discuss all of the goings on with no one else around.

What did we know about the body on the sidewalk outside Yuri's club? Apart from him working at the Russian Embassy, what was he doing in London, stamping Russian visas on Passports? How did he come by the map of the London power grid? What else was on the microchip on the pen in his pocket? Yuri had admitted to knowing him but hadn't elaborated. Did the Polish connection know that Yuri knew him? Is that why they targeted him? Did Yuri know what he was up to? Was Yuri somehow involved?

Frank and I sat there trying to figure it all out. Frank turned, scratched his nose, and said, "We need to find out more details about what O'Neill knows". We set up a meeting at Queen's Club after practice tomorrow.

We had a good training session with Michel working on his backhand chip, passing shots and drop shots. Frank and I both drilled him from the net, so he had to get ready before hitting each shot. These two on one drills were a favorite of Aussie legendary coach Harry Hopman. Of course, Yuri had a bodyguard accompany Michel as usual. O'Neill showed up just as we were coming off court. We all walked off court and up the old wooden stairs to the bar above the locker rooms. The old Queen's club was showing its age. It was in need of renovation. I felt honored to walk up those old grey wooden stairs. There was a unique sense of history that was somehow enhanced by the peeling paint and aged photographs of past champions, not just of tennis, but of the many other sports that have been hosted since its inception in 1886. It was a classic symbol of British pride and love of sports.

Frank and I sat down with O'Neill over some ice-cold beers at a quiet corner table. We ordered Carlsbergs all around. The dead man's name was Boris Umansky. He was supposedly an attaché to the Russian consulate in what they officially described as 'community outreach'. O'Neill said he was definitely engaged in spying and that MI5 believed he was seeking information on perceived terrorism targets in London. He had recently been seen with several women from Yuri's club. He was apparently sloppy with his personal affairs and had some debts to the Polish mob. That alone would have been sufficient cause for his death.

While we were listening to O'Neill, my mind kept raising the question, "Why dump a Russian spy at a mob establishment. The two generally have nothing to do with each other. As O'Neill finished filling us in with what he knew, the word terrorism stuck in my head. As an idea began to formulate, I spoke up,

"What if we have been looking at this from the wrong angle? We are assuming that this is part of a feud between two crime bosses. What if that isn't it at all? What if someone just wants us to focus on that concept to keep us from looking at something much more political in nature. We have the Tri Nations Conference coming up. Maybe this murder is just a distraction. and the unlucky victim was chosen just because he was someone

Yuri would recognize. The pen on his person was just dumb luck for us and sloppy work by his assassin."

We hashed around a bit of the current political landscape in Russia at the moment. The president was taking a lot of steps towards capitalism and was exploring a closer collaboration with Europe and possible arms agreements with the US. There was no question that there would be Russian extremists that would be very much against these moves, feeling that they were weakening their country. No matter how tight security at the conference was, an attempted terrorist attack on the Russian President was definitely a possible, even probable, reality. The more we talked about it, the more everything made sense. The information on that microchip was everything a group would need to take down security at the conference and access the President. O'Neill urgently got up to leave. He had a new focus and little time to track down assassins.

The next morning brought a drizzly, grey day and O'Neill, dressed in a grey suit, his only suit, was accompanied by his superior, the director of Scotland Yard. They entered the black front door of 10 Downing Street, passed through security, into a small entrance hall with a white tiled floor. They were greeted by the prime minister's press secretary, an older befuddled looking Englishman. He escorted them past two private secretaries into the office of the prime minister. The office looked like a throwback to the days of Winston Churchill.

O'Neill and his boss seated themselves opposite the Prime Minister's large mahogany desk in two old wingback chairs. "So, what do you have for me today gentlemen?" O'Neill came right to the point. "We have reason to believe that an extremist Russian group will attempt to assassinate the Russian president. We have some evidence that this is planned for the first day of the Tri Nations Conference". The PM took this all-in stride, "I'm sure all of our security is in place, is that so?" O'Neill chirped up, "We have everything in place, but we hope to isolate the assassins well before they reach the conference. We are in full cooperation with the Russians to be sure any attempt is averted." The PM gave him a long inquisitive look. "We just wanted to keep you informed as to what was going on. We have assigned extra uniformed and plain clothed police to conference security and alerted the Russians who have their own security teams on high alert, checking for inside personnel who could have ties to an extremist group. We already have surveillance in place around the perimeter and the power company is monitoring for any unusual activity around their substations and power controls that could be targeted, based on information on the microchip. We have even gone as far as to close off areas likely to be used by an assassin as a vantage point.

While O'Neill was meeting with the Prime Minister, he had asked that Frank and I pay a visit to our friend at the Russian Embassy. He was always glad to see us, hoping for some more tennis equipment from Frank that he could send off back home. Not to disappoint, Frank brought a gift bag with several sleeves of balls and some other sundry tennis accessories.

He wore his signature round wire rimmed glasses which magnified his bulging eyes. With his pink, puffy round face, and double chin he truly looked like a big fat bullfrog. Frank and I met with him at the Kensington Palace Hotel. He spoke fluent English and enjoyed talking with us. he liked talking about tennis and the current crop of Russian players. Frank knew him quite well, and I had chatted with him at several of the embassy parties. Frank would ensure that he would always take a large shipment of rackets and balls to sell back in Russia when he returned to Moscow.

He had guessed correctly that his wasn't just a social visit to stay in touch. We asked him what he thought about losing one of his people. He scratched his double chin, took off his glasses, attempting to clean them with a dirty handkerchief, leaned over and whispered, "it was the new Polish connection", referring to the new crime group in London. We asked "Are you sure about that? There wouldn't be any chance for a political motive for this, given the upcoming summit?" He scoffed in response as if the thought were absurd, but then stopped for a moment as if there was a thought he hadn't had a moment before. He then shook his head, "No. There would be no reason for that. I don't think so" then a quick, "Well, I'd best be getting back to work. Hope to see you at our next gathering at the embassy." He shook our hands and walked to the door with us.

We had arranged to meet up with O'Neill to report on our conversation with the ambassador. We were joined by Yuri as he wanted to hear firsthand about the Polish underground threat. We had not shared any information with him. It was up to Scotland Yard how much they wanted to share. O'Neill left it with Yuri that there was a good chance that it was more political than we thought and that it might not have been the Polish. In reality, no one had taken credit for the kill, which is somewhat unusual if the act was meant as a warning of any kind.

Frank left to meet with Lucy, and Michel and I joined Yuri in his new Black Rolls Royce to head back to his club. He was excited to show off his new wheels. As we rounded a corner near the club on the waterfront, we felt a sudden bump from the rear. The Rolls sped up with ease to avoid the car behind us and suddenly, out of nowhere, a brand new 1992 Hummer rammed the front end of the Rolls toward the river. Few vehicles on the road would have enough power to even attempt running a Rolls off the road, but this year they had just produced a civilian version of the military Humvee and it was more than up to the task. Alex had managed to avoid the trees and a few pedestrians along the esplanade and was trying to regain control of the vehicle when we were rammed by the Hummer and the front end forced into the low wall. As the hummer backed up for another hit, we braced ourselves. Michel's bodyguard, who was driving, had opened his window and was able to draw his Luger and let off a few shots at the vehicle about to ram us. The Hummer front end had been fitted with what looked like a custom designed push bar that caught the Rolls just right to send it tumbling over the wall and into the river. It seemed as if we were rolling over the wall in slow motion. It hit the water more or less on its side and the current pushed it upright before it came to rest in the shallow edge of the river.

I must've blacked out before we hit the water. The next thing I knew, a London cop was pulling me out of the car into waist deep water and there were police, rescue personnel and onlookers in complete chaos all around. As the officer helped me make my way through the muck to the stairs at Cleopatra's Needle he asked, "You au'right mate?" I answered, "I'm wet, cold, shocked and pissed off, but I'm not hurt". The Rolls was big and heavy and saved us all from serious injury. We had come to rest in about four feet of muddy water. 'That must have been the Polish connection", I thought. Yuri had a few choice words, all in Russian. He was furious! His beautiful Rolls stuck in the muddy Thames, battered, and banged up. There would be hell to pay for this, to be sure. Just what London needed, a mob war.

Yuri, Michel and Alex were already on dry ground. O'Neill had gotten the call on his radio and was just approaching as I stepped onto the esplanade. Alex, who didn't speak much English, and stuttered when he did speak, claimed that he may have wounded one of our assailants, as he said: "I g--o--t one of those bb--as--stards!" Even though it wasn't likely that a member of a mob would use public emergency services, O'Neill sent one of his men off checking local clinics and hospitals to see if they had any new admissions.

After all of us had given statements to the police and had been checked for any injuries, we were given a ride back to Yuri's club. Everyone was silent – afraid of the rage that Yuri was most definitely feeling. The bartender poured us all shots of vodka. As he was pouring the second round, I noticed him put down another glass. I turned to see Frank walking in the door. He had heard the news on the radio and had gone to the scene of the accident where they told him where I was. I was still in shock, but the adrenaline was slowly subsiding. I asked for the phone. If Frank had heard the news, chances were that Mirium had also. I needed to hear her voice and let her know I was unharmed. She answered the phone with a question and fear in her voice. All I said was "I'm OK." I heard her let out the breath she was holding. "Thank God! I was so frightened! The news didn't have any details, and they didn't know if there were any casualties or injuries, or who was in the car. All I knew was that you might be with him today." After assuring her that everything was fine and that Frank had arrived to get me back to his place, where I could rest. I handed the phone back to the bartender. I had a splitting headache and could still hear the crunching metal from the collision and feel and smell the cold, muddy Thames around my legs. My head was starting to spin, and I just wanted to lie down. I dozed on and off during the drive. The security guard at Frank's building saw us enter. He acknowledged us with a nod. "Glad to see you weren't hurt." was all he said.

I picked up a morning paper from a corner newsboy. The headlines were about the forthcoming tri summit between Britain, Russia, and the US. There was a lot of tension in London at this time, especially whenever foreign leaders meet. They were to meet at Kensington Palace.

Tennis around the world is governed by the International Tennis Federation. They are tasked with, among other things, preserving the integrity of the game. My association with a known London underworld figure has already raised some questions and concerns regarding the potential for fixing the Championship tennis matches. Roger Randall's involvement with the Italian Mafia did nothing to ease the organizations concerns. Me, being involved in any way, two days before Wimbledon opens, in the car of a Russian syndicate leader, pushed the limits of the ITF. I received a phone call the next morning, requesting my presence at their office at Baron's Court, next to the Queens club, at 11:00 am.

I checked the local news on the TV and was relieved to see that there was no footage that showed my face. I also noticed that they did not mention the name of the passengers in the car, only that it belonged to Yuri Grossegan. I had to believe that O'Neill might have been responsible for the uncharacteristic discretion of the press. When I looked through the morning paper the story was a low-key piece on the third page and the lack of details was the same.

The decision was made that, considering the training of Yuri's nephew, which was obviously a professional trainer/student relationship, my past heroics in finding the killer of Dom last year, and affidavits they had gotten from Frank, Inspector O'Neill, and Michael Ladden, my standing in the tournament was not jeopardized by the ties that I had to organized crime. They did stress that they would be scrutinizing my play, and that of Michel, very carefully.

10

It's a Mental Game

The night before my Centre Court match, I dreamt of another place and time; my first time on a Centre Court, back in Sydney, many years before.

It was a bright warm Sydney December day when I left my house in West Chatswood. I was to play a junior match in the New South Wales Championships at White City.

I checked into the junior's locker room with time to spare. I won my match, reveling in playing on the grass. Grass suited my game, although I rarely got to practice on it. After my match I decided to go over to centre court to see what was going on. Owen Davidson was playing one of my junior friends, so I took a seat in the stands to watch. As I sat down, Roy Emerson came in and sat in front of me with several of his friends. Emerson was the former Wimbledon Champion, had easy draws and won almost everything. He was very fit and could wear most of his opponents down with ease.

Tom Okker had the locker next to me and we struck up a conversation. Tom was the one who told me I was to play Roy Emerson next match on Centre Court. Tom told me Roy had a weak second serve I could exploit. He told me to hit to the corners on every second serve and come to the net.

It was about an hour before I was called for my match. I suddenly became very nervous. I had called my mum to tell her to watch me on TV on centre court against Roy Emerson, the best player in the world at that time! But that made me even more tense.

When I finally walked through the tunnel with Roy Emerson, from shade to sunny brightness my legs felt like jelly. Here I was living a dream-playing on Centre Court.

We began our warmup. First thing I noticed was, he didn't hit the ball very hard. He did have an unusual hitch on his forehand backswing which made it hard to read. The centre court was very flat with true bounces. The ball bounced higher than the outside courts. This was an early round so the court was very green and slick. I made the mistake of glancing towards the spectators. I was unnerved and excited at the same time. The TV cameras were there. While they were mostly focused on Emerson, I had to imagine that I would be in at least some of the footage. The match was to be broadcast live on ABC (the Australian Broadcasting Commission) all over Australia.

In the warmups I felt pretty good - Roy's shots were easy to handle, not overwhelming as I had expected. I tried returning his serves to the corners and they went right where I aimed. I was on! We tossed for serve and Roy elected to receive. Before that first point, I was very nervous. However, after I served that first ace, the nervousness stemming from knowing how monumental this moment was in my life, gave way to confidence. I won the first game and looked up at the scoreboard. My name was spelled incorrectly. They spelled it with two n's instead of one. There was my name up on the big scoreboard spelled HARDINGAN for all to see. At least they had Jack spelled correctly! Not to worry. I was on Centre Court, it was a great day, and I was going to enjoy myself.

When Roy started serving his first service game, I decided to swing away at every second serve. I won the game with all the kids in the stands going wild. The crowd was clearly for me - all I had to do was produce my shots and hit the corners. With the crowd roaring after every ace or return winner, I surprised myself when I hit three winners in the corners to break again, 5-2 up.

We changed ends. Roy sat down on the grass as if collecting himself. He then picked up a different racket, fiddled with the strings then changed ends with a determined look. I took some water and tried to calm myself. Hell, I was ahead. All I had to do was to keep serving as I had been doing and the first set was mine. About then, I started thinking too much. 'I'm going to beat Roy Emerson'. I became more tentative, trying not to lose my winning edge. Unfortunately, he got better. He was suddenly reading my serve much better, and I choked away several long service games.

The new strings I was using were working as I pulled off a few amazing forehands, angles and two really amazing drop shots. Hell, even Roy acknowledged them! After those shots it appeared Roy had changed his strategy though. He did not miss a shot from that point on. It appeared that he was just going to wear me down, let me go for my shots, step back and hit all my best shots back. Eventually, as this was happening, I then started to overhit and of course I started missing.

By the middle of the second set, he turned it up a notch-he started coming to net more and by the third set he was dominating. After the match we of course shook hands at the net, and he gave me a few encouraging words, which to this day I cannot remember what he said. He could have said 'better luck next time' or 'you're never going to beat Roy Emerson', but I think he said something to the effect of, 'keep trying', 'stay at it', or 'give it time'. He was known for encouraging others, especially juniors.

I woke with a start from my memories, curiously enough feeling well rested and with renewed confidence, knowing that now I had the years of experience and knowledge to play stronger and smarter than I could as a junior. The pigeons were massing again under the shade of the member's grandstand. There was a light breeze from the south and being the second day, the grass was green and slippery. I was going to have to watch my footing. My sweet lady Mirium was in the Slazenger seats with Frank and Lucy. It was a good day for tennis, and I felt great to be alive. I went into this match with nothing to lose. The last time I was on this court, only a year ago I was playing Roger Randall, brutally murdered in Milan earlier this spring, by the Sicilian Mafia. I could not help thinking on this, the brutality of his torture, how he was strung up, even though I was to play one of the greatest matches of my life. I had to remind myself this was just another match and to stick to my game plan that Frank and I had worked out. I was to play one of the legends of Wimbledon and I wanted to give a good account of myself. I had to get all outside thoughts out of my mind, just concentrate on the task at hand and play my best tennis.

11

The Match

Our plan was simple, keep the points short, down to three shots at most. This meant serving and returning with precision and beating Becker up to the net. I decided also to follow my old coach Harry Hopman's strategy for me "go for the lines". Also, as I had done before as a junior back in Australia in my first big match on Centre court, I needed to swing away as hard as I could at the corners, especially on second serves. This all meant blocking or chipping my returns and charging towards the net, get my split step set well before he struck the ball. I had to get a lot of first serves in and move forward. This was pressure tennis, making the other player rush his movements and strokes. I could smell the fresh cut moist green grass. I knew this all would work for me.

This was a warm day for London. As we progressed in the match it got hotter. My hair stuck to my head, the sun burning my arms and neck. I could feel it sting. There was not a breath of a breeze, I sat in the shade of a large umbrella at the change of ends, for a bit of relief from the sun. I would have to 'soldier on' as the Brits would say and try to concentrate on my serves and returns. In these types of situations, I always felt that I had to narrow my focus, take up a return position closer to the baseline, and try to move up into the ball and take the return of serve easily. Just focus.

Rather than focus, I found my mind wandering. Thoughts of my early days in Australia and the aborigines I taught. A nomadic people, who never stay in one place for very long. Not owning any land, they believe they are a part of the land. As such, they often go 'walkabout' to connect to that part of them. Actually, my good friend and mixed doubles partner, Evonne Goolagong (who won Wimbledon twice in the '70s, once after giving birth to her child) would often go on walkabout. Unfortunately, today, instead of focusing, I started to day-dream – I went on a mental walkabout.

Becker, on the other hand, was on top of his game today. He was all power and precision on grass, he never dropped a serve and when asked by the press "How do you serve so well under such intense pressure?" he responded simply, "Because I have to."

He was very good, negated all my tactics and countered everything with his precision and power. I learned a lot in that match, about myself and how good the top players are. He won 6-4, 6-3, 6-3.

I returned to the locker rooms mulling over the events on the court, trying to learn from my mistakes and focus on my successes. As I was changing out of my sweaty tennis clothes, I heard one of my mates holler across the locker room, "Jack, you have some friends waiting for you outside the locker room!" "Like, about, 200 women of all shapes and sizes!" he continued, laughing. I replied, "Probably all old ones," I countered, laughing also. "I am a really big hit with the over sixty crowd. They want to take me home and spoil me."

After losing the match, I wanted to walk it off. I had Frank and Lucy and Mirium go back to Frank's place. I walked and I walked, going over in my mind what I could have done better to stay focused on my game. Ironically, it seemed the more I tried to think, the less I focused. I almost ran into two boys riding bicycles along the sidewalk. The sight of them sent my mind back to my first bicycle, my red bicycle.

When I was about 10 years old my uncle gave me an old postman's bicycle he had painted red and tuned up for me.

That red bicycle was my ticket to independence and travel. I rode that bicycle everywhere and, for the first time, I had a wider horizon, which became a mantra for my life. It had become an essential part of myself - allowing me to explore and travel. And later, as a young man, I extended that travel to the world, bringing me to this point in my life.

Still thinking about how much that bike influenced the path my life had taken, I realized the sun was setting and I found myself on a darkened street. I had the sense that someone was following me. My self-talk was chastising me: "Why are you out here by yourself?" The street was deserted and very dark. The only sound was a few cars leaving a club a block or two down the street. Suddenly a pair of arms closed in around my upper body, trying to pull me backwards off balance and turning me to the right to force me down to my knees. I resisted by twisting to the left and I felt a pain in my back. The maneuver allowed me to spring away from my attacker, throwing him off balance and down onto the pavement. Without hesitation, I began to run. Thanks to my athletic upbringing, I am a pretty good runner when needed. I kept expecting the sound of a gun firing, fearful that this is how my life would end. But I just kept running. until I reached the club, where there were crowds of people, some leaving, some waiting to get in. I was shaking and breathless. The bouncers told me to move on, that I couldn't stay there. Some of those in line asked if I was OK, but others shied away, as if not wanting to get involved in whatever I had going on. I recovered my breath quickly, hailed a cab and headed back to Frank's. I realized that the attack was nothing more than a common mugger trying for an easy score on some guy stupid enough to be walking the streets alone in the dark. Keyword there – stupid.

I grabbed a cab back to Franks and joined in a pleasant evening with my friends and Mirium. I conveniently forgot to mention my excitement of the evening. Mirium was heading back home in the morning, while Frank and I planned to spend time working with Michel over at Queens.

12

Distractions

We checked in with O'Neill to see if there had been any progress in finding the hummer that had driven the Rolls into the river. He sounded frustrated. Even though the vehicle was probably the only one of its kind in all of London, especially since there were none actually registered, there had been no sign of it since the incident. Whoever it belonged to was keeping it well under wraps, holed up in some obscure garage, or even well out of the city by now. They had sent a wire through national channels to expand their search to the better part of Great Britain, but still nothing. All he could do was wait until someone decided to take it for a joyride. Yuri's contacts knew nothing about the whereabouts, but word on the street was that it had been seen out and about once or twice prior to the incident, but no one could ID the drivers. Everyone believed it was the Polish, but without a positive ID from anyone, Yuri wasn't foolish enough to start a war. Not without proof. He was a patient man when he needed to be. The vehicle would show up sooner or later, and when it did, he would deal with those responsible. They had better hope that O'Neill and his men find them first. I told O'Neill about the attack the evening before, and he said he would have one of his Bobbies in that area the next week. He repeated his previous warning to me – stay out of dark, lonely, streets.

We also asked about the summit. There had not been anything in the papers about any disturbances or trouble during the two-day event. Just the normal political analysis. Apparently, between the Russians and Scotland Yard, there was enough intel to piece together the suspected plot against the Russian President and the

Russians were able to pre-empt the attack. O'Neill managed to keep it out of the papers. As usual, the general public was blissfully unaware of how close the world came to a major political catastrophe, which could have ended in another world war.

We left practice at Queen's Club. Michel and I were in the back seat of Frank's Rover. Frank was driving. Michel's bodyguard, Alex, was in the front seat. All of a sudden, Alex yelled out, "That's the cc—ar!" Sure enough, he had spied the vehicle that had forced us off the road. Alex let out a scream, drew his Lugar, and yelled, "Let's g-get the bb-aa-st-ards". Frank made a hard right turn, cutting off an oncoming car. Not too surprisingly, there were no plates on the Hummer ahead of us. but, as O'Neill mentioned, there were none registered in London. We were following along a quiet one-way street with virtually no pedestrian traffic. Frank yelled, "Hang on!" and gunned the engine of the Rover. He flew up just ahead of the Hummer on the driver's side, catching the driver and passenger completely by surprise. Alex turned, aimed, then shot out the two front tires. The driver slammed on his brakes to get control of the vehicle, as it threatened to turn over. Frank cut the wheel and blocked the road ahead of them, as Alex jumped out and leveled his gun at them. I shouted out, "Don't shoot them! It's not worth it!" They sat in their seats with their hands in the air, looking scared senseless. Something told me they weren't supposed to be out driving the car. If that was true, they would be glad to be taken into custody by the cops. It was a better fate than facing their boss. I ran to the corner phone booth and called O'Neill. He said a car was already on the way. A tenant in one of the flats on the street had called in that a Rover and Hummer were having a shootout on her street. The police arrived before I had even hung up the phone. Frank grabbed the camera he kept in his glove box to get a picture of the two thugs. We would now let O'Neill take it from there. Yuri would handle it on his end in his own way.

We answered a few questions and were allowed to leave. We took Alex and Michel to the club, where Yuri was waiting. "Did you get them?" was his first words to Alex. Alex looked at me as I interrupted with "Michel, Frank and I would have been witnesses." Yuri's hard stare, as he turned to look at me, was unnerving, but he slowly softened his gaze as he realized that the situation would have been messy had Alex knocked off the two in the car with us standing there. Frank stepped forward with the Polaroid shots he had gotten of the two. Yuri smiled in appreciation and handed the photos to an associate standing behind him. Without a word, the man turned and left, clearly on a mission.

Yuri poured two shots of vodka "to calm the nerves" and had a soda brought for Michel. We threw back the shots, thanked him and excused ourselves. I was getting used to the fact that when it came to vodka and Yuri, any time was a good time. As we were walking out, I turned, and jerking my head in Michel's direction, said" By the way, he's looking good!" Even in the dimly lit room I would see Michel beaming.

I felt that after the experience of the day, Michel could use a change in scenery, so I suggested that he spend a couple of days up at Winston Gardens, where we could practice uninterrupted and undistracted. I took the train up to meet Mirium and prepare her for Michel's arrival. I apologized for not asking her first, but it was a spur of the moment thought. She didn't mind at all. I just kept thinking, "God I love this woman!". I spent the next day and a half working Michel hard on the courts. The second afternoon was spent at the pool and hot tub, drilling him on his mental game. I told him to spend the next day with relatively easy workouts at the gym, some running and a swim. Nothing too strenuous, just keep the body in motion and the muscles warm, not burning. I also told him to focus. Keep mentally going over his stokes, visualizing them with all the details, following the ball, carefully placing his feet, keeping his wrist firm…I felt good about him as he drove down the driveway to head home.

Finally, Mirium and I had some time to ourselves, with no one else around. It was like getting to know each other on a first date, except this wasn't a first date and we didn't have to stand on protocol. Let's just say that it was an exciting evening, ending in us sleeping in until late in the morning.

We sat together that evening, enjoying the cool air of twilight. It was as if time stood still. When I looked around, I thought back to my life on the edge of the outback. The dusty smell of dry grass and the pale green eucalyptus trees reaching to a clear blue sky, their shedding trunks with the leaves quivering in a light breeze. We were sitting outside on the balcony away from the houselights. Overhead the sky was darkening and looked like a brimming treasure chest. This was an unusually clear night for this part of England. We felt we could almost touch the stars one by one.

Mirium shut her eyes then opened them again. The whites of her eyes were clear despite the wine. I watched the angles of her cheekbones and the small dimple on her chin. I had learned to tell when she needed to say something by her subtle signals that something was bothering her. I just sat still and quiet until she was ready to speak what was on her mind.

When she did speak, she began talking of her deceased husband. She said he was much older than her and already a wealthy man when they had met. She spoke of how he took her to South Africa and of the mines, of the poverty and exploitation of the native miners and how she loved the national parks. She said that she could have had everything with him—devotion, fidelity, travel, children. She said she was quite happy with him for a long time. She had even managed to deal with his drinking and enjoyed it more and more when he was away in Africa. As his holdings in South Africa became more time consuming, she saw less of him. He had just started breeding racehorses on a large property in Kenya and loved to be there rather than at Winston Gardens. He died there of a heart attack at age 52, riding his favorite stallion in the bush, and that was that. Suddenly Mirium found herself the sole heir to his fortune, strewn on several continents. She said that she is still finding more of his holdings that she never knew about. The diamond business had been good to them both.

The next day was to be Michel's first match at Wimbledon. As one of Britain's top juniors now, the committee had given him a wildcard into the main draw. I had called him earlier and he appeared a bit on edge. I told him I would be there in the morning to give him a good warmup. His uncle and benefactor was to be there which made him more apprehensive than usual. I planned on arriving early for warmups to help him settle any pre-match jitters. I told him to treat it just like any other match. However, we both knew that this was different. Every telly in Britain would be focused on the new future star. By the look of the sky, good dry weather was promised, and a capacity crowd would be there. Yuri insisted he would be there, just what we needed, a little more pressure!

When we arrived at the main Wimbledon gates on Church Road there was a long line of those waiting to purchase grounds passes. Some had camped out the night before so as to get a space at the front of the queue. The Brits seem to love to queue! The outside streets literally pulsed with cabs and red double decker buses as they disgorged all shapes, colours, and sizes of humanity. This was to be a special day for everyone, one that evoked vivid memories for years to come. The smell of sweat and bus fumes filled the air. The whole scene just throbbed in anticipation.

The gates would not open until 10:30am and there would be a mad rush of humanity for spectators to get to their preferred spots on the outside courts. Play would not start on the outside courts until noon, to let the grass courts dry out, the main show courts including Centre Court and Court 1 would start at 2pm. However, with the long twilight, play would continue until about 9pm. Grounds passes were very inexpensive and much sought after. During the first week, with a grounds pass, patrons could see most of the top players in matches or on the practice courts and great doubles and mixed doubles until the curtain of darkness descended. It was also possible to secure a ticket after 5pm from tickets from earlier in the day that were turned back in. Proceeds from these were donated to charity. This allowed those who worked in the city to catch a train and see perhaps several hours of late day play and help one of their charities.

When I arrived, I found him in the locker room pacing the floor in his socks like a caffeinated tiger. He was obviously nervous and in some distress. This was not just his usual pre-match jitters. He clearly had something more on his mind. At that moment Frank pulled me aside and said with some urgency. "Michel's new girlfriend is here in the stands!" "That would explain everything" I said to Frank. I immediately remembered my "Inner Game" strategies from Timothy Gallway. I hustled him out to the courts for a good warmup. I also had Frank go and find the new girlfriend and bring her courtside to view our warm-ups on an outside court. This seemed to ease all the tension. We hit for about an hour, he got up a good sweat and had a chance to talk with his girl.

As soon as I laid eyes on the girlfriend, I could see what all the fuss was about. Her name was Kim, a real knockout blonde, settling onto the courtside bench with a comfortable curvy wiggle. This was to be another challenge!

Michel's first match was to be on Court 1. After sorting out 'the new girlfriend thing' Michel started off a little jittery but finally made a good match of it, losing to the fourth seed in four tight sets. Everybody, including the press, said that he showed off his talent. However, I thought he made too many errors of stroke and judgement.

From the first roar of the crowd, expectations of players and spectators alike, the points as they are played at Wimbledon, are quick, transient, ephemeral things. Match momentum can change in an instant on one key point, especially on grass courts. Indeed, that was what happened at 4-4, forty thirty in the fourth set. Michel's opponent hit one great running passing shot for a winner at just the right time.

13

Vacation

Before leaving for Lausanne, at Mirium's suggestion, we drove over to Oxford. At Oxford, I planned to do my post-doctoral studies reading in Humanism. I was interested in helping people find themselves through sports, probably a little wacko for most philosophy profs at Oxford. We were in awe of the five centuries of history and the historic architecture, vine covered walkways and the many worn stone steps where the great scholars had walked. However, I did find one prof in the Psychology department who had researched Humanism and read widely in the psychology and sociology of sports. He had seen me play on TV at Wimbledon and agreed to take me on. I was admitted as a postdoc for the Fall. I agreed to meet with my prof once a month. He gave me a letter to get me into the archive collections for libraries in Venice, Florence and Rome. He gave me several books to read on my travels including summaries of the works of Plato, Socrates, Bacon, and the works of Petrarch (1304-1375), his sonnets and letters. He also encouraged me to read again the more contemporary works of George Herbert and Margaret Mead.

Humanism stresses the potential value and goodness in human beings, emphasizing common human needs and seeks rational ways of teaching and solving human problems. A philosophical stance that emphasizes the individual and social potential of human beings. This ties in with my work developing Natural Movement and Personalized Learning models which I started at the Universities of Sydney, and Oregon and last summer at the

University of London. As we were driving back, she put her hand on my knee and said, "We'll need an extra travel bag for all your books!".

We arrived in Lausanne, a city on the northern shores of Lake Geneva, in the late afternoon. Our jet's approach path took us over the water and the sun's angle created an appearance of a million diamonds glistening on the surface of the water. There was a car waiting for us. Traffic was a bit heavy at that time of day and the ride to the hotel took us about 20 minutes, driving along one-way streets, through the downtown areas lined with businesses and parked motor scooters, navigating around the electrified trolleybuses, and down the steep hills. The architecture along our route was mostly unremarkable, the typical combination of old and new. We made a very short stop at the bank to check on the status of the move. We were told it had not occurred yet, and that it was bank policy not to disclose the actual date the move was planned – security protocol and all. As we approached our hotel, the Royal Savoy Hotel & Spa, the view was mostly blocked by trees, with the exception of the spires along the roof line, which gave a hint to the magnificent edifice that lies beneath.

We arrived after most of the new guests had checked in and before the dinner crowd had emerged from their rooms, so the lobby was relatively empty. You could hear muffled conversation and the clink of glasses from a solitary couple in the intimate lounge area. From our hotel the views were spectacular with the Alps in the background. We unpacked the basics and decided to take a long walk along the lake. We found a wonderful Swiss restaurant near our hotel. It was good to be outdoors walking in the long twilight.

The wind had blown a veil of clouds about, and the sun was just suspended above the horizon in a spherical orange blur. We paused again and gazed at the reflections on the waves brushing the pebbled beach shoreline.

After our long day we were getting hungry. We elected to go to one of the small restaurants by the shore. The one we chose was famous for their Coq au Vin and their selection of local wines.

We entered the restaurant. Tchaikovsky's 1812 Overture was playing in the background. Mirium was the main attraction. As we drifted in, everyone turned in their seats to get a better view, with good reason. She wore a long, black sequined cocktail dress, low cut in the front and back. Her long, slender legs flashed out from under her long skirt. She walked in with a straight back and a confident smile as we were led in by the maître d'. Her eyes sparkled like stars in the dim candlelight. Some of the women eyed her sparkling, jeweled necklace, leaning toward each other to whisper jealous comments. I decided to embrace the moment. Here I was again with this beautiful, intelligent, attractive woman. I decided to soak it all up.

Out of habit, at this point, I was vigilant about our surroundings, despite the fact that there was no reason to be concerned for our safety. I had not detected anyone following us, which was a pleasant change. When our first course arrived, we found it difficult to show some restraint and not act as if this was our first meal in days. Finally, being free from stress and fear allowed our minds to take in the gastronomical pleasures of a leisurely meal and our appetites kicked into high gear, beginning with crusty French bread right through to the finishing touch of a crisp vegetable salad in the French tradition, then a small raspberry tart for dessert. Life felt very good.

Sleeping that night without stress was also a treat, and Mirium next to me made it a slice of heaven.

The morning view from our hotel revealed a clear and fresh mountain day. I could see snow on the Alps in the distance as I walked down to the local tennis club. It was early on a Saturday morning and there appeared to be some kind of junior tournament going on. I instantly recognized one of my old mates from junior tennis in Australia. He said he was coaching there at one of the clubs and playing league tennis for the club, sponsored by a local brewery. He was given a place to stay and a nice stipend to coach and compete for them.

As we walked around, we observed a slightly built teenager. He said "Oh, that's Roger". He took a pause, "he's one of our better juniors in his age group now, but a bit hot headed, loses his temper a lot!" We watched a bit longer. He moved with a certain grace and ease, had a good forehand and serve for his age, but his backhand needed work. His second serve was a bit weak too. He was gliding to the ball all right but his stepping to his one-handed backhand was all out of sync. It seemed like his backhand grip was a bit off too. I suggested to my friend Peter that "he needs to do away with that big step before he hits his backhand". He could hit a decent slice and slice approach shot but had no reliable power on his backhand. Further, "If he wants to develop a really good flat or topspin backhand drive, he needs to eliminate that big step before he hits it. I later found out by looking at the names on the junior boys' draw, his name was Roger Federer.

That night at dinner we mulled over our travel options. Mirium wanted to visit with some art dealers in Venice and feel out options for selling the van Gogh. She had made some calls before we left and all of the dealers were out of town at a convention for the next few days, so there was no reason to hurry. We could play tourist along the route and take some side trips.

We had dinner at Lacustre by the lake. It was a short walk from our hotel, The Royal Savoy Lausanne. As we walked down the hill, we could see that it had a lively outdoor bar overlooking Lake Geneva. A four-piece smooth-jazz band played favorites for an international clientele. According to the restaurant guide in our room at the hotel, 'it provided fine international fare with an award-winning French chef'. When we arrived, the dining room was full. The ambiance was just what we were looking for and the food we saw go by on trays heading to the various patrons looked exceptional, so we accepted the offer of a small bar table by the rail on the lake until our table was ready. From this vantage, we had an unobstructed view of the beautiful crimson sunset over the lake. The bar offered a bottle of champaign to whoever could guess the exact time the sun disappeared beyond the horizon. This appeared to be a daily tradition here and the reason the bar was overfull. After sunset people started leaving, the winners, a happy local couple disappeared, chattering gleefully on their way down the steps, seemingly melting into the clear, cool twilight.

Mirium had found out from a local couple we had met that Lausanne has a quaint old medieval city centre and a 12th century Gothic cathedral. Lausanne, long known for its political stability, banking, and hospitality is also the headquarters of the International Olympic Committee which houses a spectacular Olympic Museum. Another trip to plan in the future. Our future. A concept I was growing very comfortable with.

As the crowded bar thinned, our waiter came for us and said "Your table is ready" in English. We moved inside to a very elegant corner table for two. The seats were like lounge chairs, covered in velvet, lights were dimmed with an antique candelabra and local wildflowers on the table. Mirium murmured to me "Well worth the wait" and "perfect for a romantic evening". She took my hand, looked into my eyes, kissed my fingers.

At Lacustre they had a very international menu. Our waiter was French but spoke good English. He suggested we start with the pate then a rabbit consommé, specialty of the chef, cooked in the French style. Sounded good to me. I had the rabbit; Mirium ordered the local fish. Hers came with the great crisp pomme frites. I ate most of them. We had a nice bottle of Swiss mountain white wine, recommended by the in-house sommelier, and shared one of their Swiss pastries from the mobile tray. As we left, we stopped and paused on the balcony together for a long, lingering look at the scene, as if trying to memorize this moment in time, forever. The next morning, we would be heading on to Venice.

14

Our Journey Begins

We had decided to take the train from Lausanne to Venice. The opportunity to be immersed in the scenery and terrain of the Swiss and Italian Alps was just too compelling compared to the prospect of the relatively two-dimensional view one gets from flying over them. As the train schedules worked out, we would meander through Switzerland, heading northeasterly to Bern then turning south and a bit east toward Milan, Italy. There our path would be turning due east to Venice. The trip as planned would only take one day. It did however mean that we had to be at the station very early in the morning, as our train would be leaving at 6:18 am.

The station in Lausanne was, as most of the city, very old architecture and quite large. The interior had the standard seating, rows of straight benches with areas of s-shaped back-to-back benches to break up the monotony. The ceiling was high with large fans to help circulate the somewhat musty air that is so prevalent in older buildings. We chose to sit in the curved benches, just to make it easier to chat about our plans for the trip. One wall of the massive hall was dotted with ticket agents behind iron barriers, sorting through the process of getting people from point A to point B as efficiently as possible, while accommodating all of the little pet peeves and changes and special requirements that travelers can be known to have. We were no different, since, as we were sitting there, the tourist brochures in the attractions rack caught our eye and we simultaneously began to say, "We should…" Our sentence was cut short as we both began to laugh at the synchronicity of our thoughts. Mirium got up from the bench and after scanning all of the possibilities in the rack, came back to sit beside me with a brochure for Bolzano, a history rich town in Italy north of Verona, which she thought would make a nice stop before facing the business in Venice. It seems that on a previous trip, she had learned about Bolzano from a couple of young Swiss students who were spending their summer exploring, hiking and enjoying the good local food and wine.

It was a short trip but would require a layover before returning to Verona and then on to Venice.

Mirium went to one of the ticket agents who was free and booked our little side trip. We would arrive in Bolzano at 10:31 am, in time to plan our afternoon, and get a start on seeing the sights before lunch. We planned to sightsee as much as possible before heading back to Verona and on to Venice. We sat there going through the brochure, trying to identify the hotel the students Mirium had spoken with had recommended and used one of the many payphones to call ahead for a reservation for 1 night. The arrangements were completed just in time for the first boarding call for our train. Many of the people who had been sitting around us got up and headed towards our track.

With each little village and hamlet, we passed through, there was the almost deafening blast of our train's horn, the sound reflecting off of the wall of mountains surrounding us as we passed over, around or through the solid rock faces. I noted how quiet the train wheels were on the tracks. Most of the rails in Europe had been welded continuous rail since the mid '50s, but had only become widespread in Britain during the '60s. Most people still associated the thought of rail travel with the click clack of the wheels as they passed over the seams in the old rails. That sound had been romanticized by movies as the way trains sound, and I think we still hear it in our minds, even if it is no longer true. In the main dining car, our conversation was light and filled with laughter, as we set aside the main purpose of our trip and just enjoyed the sights, sounds and sensations of the train ride. At times our conversation mingled with others, as most of the inhabitants of the car seemed to be in the mood for revelry. There were two men in the far corner who seemed determined to not let the festive air penetrate their gloom. They were obviously not on a pleasure trip. I sensed that they didn't understand the concept of pleasure. As my eyes returned to lock with Mirium's gaze, an involuntary smile came to my lips. I quickly forgot the gloomy twosome and reveled in the love radiating from her face.

One of the groups on the train was on an excursion to Belalp mountain via the cable car from Blatten Bei Naters. Since it would only mean a few hours delay before the next train came through heading to Milan, we allowed ourselves to be talked into the side trip up the mountain. We had planned on taking a cable car when in Bolzano, but this would free up our time to do other sightseeing we also wanted to do. It was a very spontaneous decision, and we hastily gathered our luggage and deboarded the train at Brigs. We hopped off just as the train whistle announced its departure. I had bent over to pick up our luggage and as I stood erect, I noticed the two gloomy men were frantically running towards the door of the train, pointing in our direction. I watched as the train rapidly accelerated out of the station, with the two men glaring out the window. I looked towards Mirium and saw that she was preoccupied with arranging her belongings and smoothing her hair, which had gotten a bit mussed by our hasty departure. She had not noticed the men, and I decided it was best not to mention them. I did, however, start paying more attention to our fellow travelers.

I was just an average skier, but the moment I saw the powdery slopes on the peaks that surrounded Brig, I couldn't resist the temptation to ski in Switzerland! It was not winter season, but at the higher elevations, even summer was not a deterrent to snow covered slopes and glacier skiing. Once again, we made a hasty decision to alter our plans, opting to forgo the cable car. Instead, we set our sights on Zermatt, to the south, which overlooks the peak of the Matterhorn. One of the many mountains which typically had skiing all year long on at least some of the slopes, it did not disappoint this year. There was a train that ran all day long between Brig and Zermatt, but we had had enough sitting on the train seats and opted to rent a more comfortable Land Rover for the 23-mile trek up to the mountain. We also didn't want to spend the extra time the train would have taken. As we traveled on the road leading up to Zermatt, we began postulating how Van Gogh would portray the scene before our eyes. As we huddled close together in the car, she commented that, no matter how many times she had traveled through the Alps, she was always held in awe of the overpowering majesty of these peaks that made one realize the unimaginable forces that had formed them. In stark contrast to the huge boulders in the scene, we passed several goat herds, and these small, simple animals had learned to master moving around these seemingly unsurpassable rock formations with the light agility of ballet dancers on a stage. Our vehicle navigated the steep and winding ascent without giving us any cause for concern about our safety, despite the somewhat slushy surface.

As it turns out, Mirium is an elite skier. After all of the sitting for the last couple of days of travel, she became positively giddy from the exercise, not to mention the chance to show off her moves to me. When we stopped after several hours of exploring the trails, her entire body seemed to be glowing from the fresh air and exertion. I couldn't help but get caught up in her mood as I grasped her around the waist and spun her around me in a circle, both of us laughing like a couple of school kids. We stopped off at the Chalet for some warm spiced cider to help chase off the chill of the mountain air, before hopping back in the Land Rover for the drive back down to Brig to catch the next train.

As we approached our rental, still chatting and laughing as if we didn't have a care in the world, my eye caught sight of a black BMW SUV, complete with tinted windows. The kind you would see in a spy movie. I only noticed it because it was parked away from most of the cars and stuck out against the white snow backdrop. It also had the engine running and two men sitting in the front seats, looking our way. This time, when I turned towards

Mirium, she had seen my glance and was turning to look in the same direction. I scooped her towards me and gave her a long, loving kiss before she could notice the SUV. It was enough of a distraction that she forgot what she was going to look at, and, smiling sweetly at me, she got into our vehicle. I got into the driver's seat, but not without another look at the SUV. The men in it were definitely watching us and I could see the reflection of the brake lights in the snow behind the vehicle as the driver depressed the brake pedal. They were ready to start moving.

As we pulled out of the parking lot I was beginning to wish we had taken the train up here. At least the road had dried since we drove up. I kept glancing at the rear view for the BMW, and, as I suspected, I saw them come up to the car behind us. There was some other traffic on the road, a couple of cars ahead of us and one behind. Mirium must have noticed I seemed a bit tense and caught me glancing in the mirror. She turned in her seat to look behind us. It was hard not to notice the hulk of the SUV. She let out a short gasp and her head snapped to look at me. I was focused on the road, but gave a little nod to indicate that, yes, I did know about the SUV and yes, we were being followed. My plan was to try to lose them in the streets of Zermatt before we began the 2000' descent down to Brig. I sped up and the car behind us allowed me to get far enough ahead to round a curve and take a quick left onto a side street, while out of sight of the BMW. Straight would have led to a dead end. I gunned the engine and made the next right, hoping to get far enough that once our tail managed to turn around and continue in pursuit we would be completely out of sight. We were in a residential neighborhood with a winding road leading up the side of the mountain. We could see the road we needed to get to in order to head to Brig below us. We could also see the SUV we were trying to avoid, and it appeared they saw us. I turned around when I could and headed back down the hill to hopefully get behind our pursuers. We did not see them anywhere and were praying that we had actually lost them. We drove slowly toward the edge of town, wishing there was more than one road leading back. We passed the town limits with no sign of the SUV. There were several pull offs that afforded storage and rest areas for trucks and after passing several, we were beginning to think we were in the clear. From the other side of the road, I saw the unmistakable front bumper of the BMW as it bolted out trying to ram us. I slammed on the brakes and the vehicle just missed our front end, coming to a stop before smashing into a group of trees off the road. I swerved around it and took advantage of the Land Rover's power to put some distance between us as the other driver backed up and got back on the road. There was no place for us to try to lose them and the Rover was no match for the acceleration of the BMW. I was able to pass a slow truck in front of me just before a curve, which bought us a few brief moments, before the BMW was back on our tail. They were trying to pull to our left and I kept swerving to deter them. The road was getting steeper and more winding as we continued and I was forced to focus on where I was going, not on what they were doing. Between the curves and the occasional oncoming traffic, we had a bit of a standoff, until we came onto a short straight stretch of road and the BMW gunned their engine to come up on our left. I was ready to ram their front end. I was not ready for the gun in the hand of the passenger aimed at me. I yelled at Mirium to "Get down! He has a gun!"

I slammed on the brakes, again, just as a shot rang out and the driver's side window shattered. By some miracle I was not hit. I screamed at Mirium "Are you OK?" and she shouted back "Yes!"

I remembered a tunnel on our way up and spotted a sign for it coming up ahead after a curve. The gunmen fell back again for another pass. I hit the gas and began blocking their path again. As we approached the entrance to the tunnel, I intentionally let them start passing me. With a quick turn of the wheel, I pushed their front end to the left just as we reached the tunnel abutment. The Rover may not have been as fast as they were, but they were no match for the raw power behind my turn. Their car smashed head on into the side of the tunnel entrance, bursting into an explosion of flames, broken glass and twisted metal. We exited the other end, still at high speed, as I tried to maintain control of our vehicle. Less than a half mile after the tunnel was a pull off. We parked there, people looking at us very strangely, with our broken window and banged up front end, but when they gave us questioning looks, they respected our nod and wave as a sign that we didn't want to talk to anyone right then. We didn't linger. The last thing we wanted was to start being questioned about the wreck we left behind. We had no choice but to continue along the only road to Brig. We somehow managed to get back without any further drama. We were both very quiet along the way. We told the rental car company that we had hit a deer and the antler took out the driver's window. The agent marked down the damage and dismissed us without any other questions. I guess it was no skin off of his back. He just worked there. We checked our bags, used the restrooms to freshen up a bit and went into the coffee shop. It was full of tourists, teens, backpackers, and parents with small children. It all seemed so normal. We couldn't remember life being normal. I headed over to one of the pay phones and pulled out Michael Ladden's phone number. There was no answer, and his machine was full. I rejoined Mirium and we sat in the small café. We sipped our espresso and put our empty cups down just in time to gather our luggage and get on the next train out. As the train pulled from the station, our eyes locked, disbelief shrouding our thoughts. Mirium gave a small, pathetic giggle, which I returned with an ever so slight smile. Her giggle turned into a smile, which in turn became a nervous laugh. I couldn't help myself, and I began to laugh along with her. The other riders in the car must have thought we had lost our minds, as we laughed out loud for several minutes, finally regaining our composure as the adrenaline rush of the last hour finally wore off.

15

Why Are They Trying to Kill Us?

There were many new faces and fresh conversations on this leg of the trip. The acquaintances we had made before our trip up the mountain had all caught the train back north, and a new group were now heading in our direction. This time I was on the lookout for anyone who didn't seem to fit in with the rest of the travelers. It was a very mixed group. Most fell either into the category of young revelers or old fun-loving travelers. No one stood out like the grumpy two on the first leg of the trip.

We continued our journey down to Milan without incident and I began to feel like the events earlier were just a bad dream. We talked about the attempt on our lives and could not come up with any reason that someone would try to kill us. Not even my relationship with Yuri would be enough of a reason for us to be targeted. Especially here in Switzerland. The only explanation that seemed to make any sense was that we had been mistaken for someone else. Maybe we were just grasping at straws, neither of us wanting to believe that anyone wanted us dead. We had a short wait for our train to Verona, during which Mirium made the changes to our trip to Bolzano, based on our new arrival time in Verona. Since we would be getting in late in the day, we decided to overnight in Verona to give us some time to sightsee. As we left the station and began the journey east, we passed through the main rail yard in the eastern outskirts of Milan. I couldn't help but notice the seemingly endless line of container trucks boasting the San Pellegrino water brand, which happened to be a favorite of mine. I mentioned it to Mirium, and she informed me that the source for Pellegrino's sparkling mineral water was about 60 km northeast of Milan. We had to assume by the trucks that there was no rail line that went directly to their facility. We made a note to take a trip there someday, assuming we survived this trip. Apparently, there was quite a nice spa that would not be as crowded as mainstream resorts and spas you find in more populated areas in Italy. Boy, did that sound good right about now.

It was only about an hour and a half to Verona, where we would catch a train to Bolzano. There was a mid-aged gentleman sitting near us who was sipping his wine and seemed to be enjoying watching the young revelers in the car, as if they were bringing back fond memories of a younger man. As we were looking through the brochures and discussing what we would do there, he overheard our mention of Bolzano and immediately turned his attention to our conversation. In broken English, he excused himself for being nosey, and inquired if we were planning a trip to Bolzano. He said he had spent many summers there with his wife before she passed away from cancer. It held many fond memories. He asked if we were planning on touring the town. Upon hearing that we had just planned to do some 'tourist' sightseeing, he adamantly shook his head with his brow creased and wagged his finger in front of us with a hearty "no, no, no". "You must visit this spot" he said as he pulled out a pad of paper and pen from his jacket pocket (Europeans always seem ready to write down directions). "It is a view that will leave you breathless!" he insisted with the requisite accentuation of the last statement with hand gestures. He spoke a bit more about his wife and then, it seemed that he needed a change in the subject, and he excused himself to go chat and laugh with 'the revelers' as we had begun to call them.

The trip across northern Italy was full of beautiful views of the Alps, green valleys, what seemed like medieval castles on every mountain top and lots of olive trees and vineyards. The sun was getting lower in the sky and glistened off of everything it touched, making many of the buildings appear to be made of gold. We were already almost to Verona, and we gathered our belongings in preparation for getting off the train. We wished that we had traveled a bit lighter by this point. Verona was a large enough station to have facilities to store baggage. We checked most of our larger bags to lighten our load for the side trip. As we were heading out to the track our next train was on, we passed by the gentleman we had spoken with on the train. He was on the phone, but when he saw us, his face brightened, he interrupted his conversation, and we got a big smile and exuberant thumbs up as he shouted "Bolzano!" It was heartwarming how fond memories that we make during life can lift one's spirits. We smiled and waved back, shouting "One night in Verona, first!" He responded "Ah, good! OK, OK," and went back to his conversation.

It was early evening and there was a lot of traffic, as we made our way by cab to our hotel. We were both a bit on edge, warily watching the traffic for anything that looked suspicious. Verona is in the Valpolicella valley and is famous for its first century Roman amphitheater and its local wine. It is the city chosen by Shakespeare as the site for two of his plays, even though he had supposedly never been there. Tourists flock to Juliet's balcony off the square, to see a daily show each day in the summer. This was adding to the traffic.

We checked into our hotel, and I tried calling Ladden again. Still no answer. We freshened up a bit and then wandered around the old city of Verona, just enjoying the lingering warmth from a perfect sun-drenched afternoon. We stopped for a glass of wine and some light pastries at a corner café to give our feet a rest. The softness of the late afternoon shadows brought welcome relief to our exhausted minds as we continued on our way. Following cues from the brochure we had read, we came up to the Roman ruins. We stopped walking and listened, turning toward each other with puzzled looks. We were hearing familiar music, in English. There happened to be a large crowd inside the ancient amphitheater. Instead of deadly gladiatorial games as in Roman times, the City of Verona put on a concert once a month. We went in. We were in for a treat. Cliff Richard, about the most popular singer in Britain and Europe at this time was just getting started. We listened to very familiar music which was in sharp contrast to the ancient architecture which surrounded us. It gave the sensation of having passed through some sort of time/space portal. He started with "Mistletoe and Wine", then to "The Best of Me". The crowd loved it all. The show was a special fundraiser for UNESCO titled "The Music of Cliff Richard", celebrating years of hit singles. The many lovers in the audience cuddled up to his signature song, "Please Don't Fall in Love", getting lost in every minute of it. As a crimson sunset filled the sky the ancient stones behind the stage took on the same pinkish hue.

As we filed out with the happy crowd, we reflected on how great this day was ending. We both felt like we had been on a roller coaster ride of adrenaline all day. Having been near death at gunpoint earlier that day made such an enchanting evening seen even more spectacular. However, I had this odd feeling in my stomach that something was not quite right. After leaving the concert, we stopped at a restaurant which seemed to be the local favorite après concert hangout. Even though we were tired, the noise from laughter and conversation seemed just right after the concert. As we headed out to return to our hotel, I thought that one of the waiters seemed to be taking note of us leaving. I shook my head and told myself to stop being so paranoid, but that didn't help the feeling of being tracked.

We returned to the hotel where we were staying. As we entered the room, it appeared as if our room had been searched. Nothing was taken, all of our cash, jewelry, passports were in the hotel safe or inside my money belt, but our luggage was not exactly where we remembered leaving it and had been left unlatched with zippers partially open. The contents were not as neatly folded as both of us are accustomed to doing. One of the dresser drawers wasn't quite closed all of the way. We called down to the front desk to ask if housekeeping had been in our room and they assured us no one from the hotel staff had entered while we were out. We explained why we were asking, and they seemed to pass off our concern as just some tourists who couldn't remember how they left their room. We decided not to file a formal report with the authorities but became more vigilant in our movements. The question in our minds was whether this was just a random event of local thieves looking for cash, jewelry, or drugs, or was it somehow connected to the unexplained events earlier that day. I tried Ladden again and still no answer. I called O'Neill's number and left a message that he would get in the morning, telling him we were trying to reach Ladden. The machine cut the message off before I added any details.

We had room service bring up some coffee in the morning as we prepared to catch our train. As we left our room, I vaguely thought I heard the phone ringing, but Mirium was speaking, and I didn't want to interrupt her. As we checked out, we inquired at the front desk as to whether any other guests reported suspicious activity or possible intrusion into their room. The desk clerk seemed offended at the idea and gave us a curt "No! Of course not!" He turned and went into the back office, since clearly our business with him was complete before I could ask if we had any messages.

Rail travel affords great views of small towns and the everyday locals going about their business. We enjoyed a hearty breakfast in the dining car offering local favorites and fresh foods from the region we were passing.

In Bolzano we debarked the train with a few tourists and a handful of businessmen who were apparently returning from a flight into Verona from elsewhere in Europe. Similar to regional airports in the US which only accept domestic flights, Valerio Catullo Airport in southeastern Verona only handled flights from elsewhere in Europe. We were both nervously sizing up everyone we saw. No one had given us a second look.

We went straight to our hotel to arrange to have our bags held until we could check in later. The bags were being delivered from the station. Although normal check-in wasn't until late afternoon, we were able to pay for an early check-in. It would just take an hour to have the room ready, so we took a short walk around the square, bought a bottle of local wine and some sandwiches from a local cafe to enjoy once the room was ready.

We also were fortunate and got one of their best suites with an old wrought iron balcony overlooking the local green vineyards in one direction, the Alps in the other. The old balcony was vintage 1912, much of the cream paint on the outside walls was peeling, but the view was spectacular. We pulled the two chairs together on the balcony, so we could sit close and enjoy an intimate lunch with our wine and sandwiches. The wine was a mountain wine called Teroldego, made from grape vines on mountain slopes facing south, picked late in the year, rich in body and flavor. We had passed through the area on our way here. We liked it so much that when we left our room later, we stopped off at the shop where we had purchased it and had several cases sent back to Winston Gardens.

We read the maps and brochures about the area given to us at check in. Thankfully much of these were in English and the front desk gave us a local map of walking trails, local restaurants and special points of interest within walking distance. We decided to take the recommended public walking path the next day, which winds up the slopes with special views of the vineyards and wildflowers leading up to a local winery open for lunch.

According to the brochures, Bolzano was in the South Tyrol Region of Northern Italy. This was the gateway to the Italian Alps, very popular with skiers in the late fall and winter. It was famous for its medieval city centre and of course 'Otzi the Iceman'. Otzi is an ancient, ice-preserved Tyrolian hunter mummified from 5,000 years ago, along with his hunting bow, arrowheads, and travel satchel. We could find him on exhibit at the Tyrol Museum of Archaeology across the square from our hotel. The front desk told us to get there a half hour before it opened in the morning to avoid the lines and that it was a 'must see'. There was much to see and do including the thirteenth century Mareccio Castle a few miles up the mountain, and the Duomo di Bolzano Cathedral with its classic Romanesque and Gothic architecture, fine art, tapestries, and ancient relics preserved by the church. As a border community with one of the shortest distances through Austria to Germany, both German and Italian were spoken.

We opted for a guided tour of the 13th century French Gothic Cathedral's grounds. As we were crossing the grounds between the Cathedral and its gardens, we happened upon a group of monks in their long brown robes, who were playing an ancient handball game. They called it 'jue de palm' or game of the hand. Our Duomo guide said that the monks had been playing this same authentic game since the 14th century. The game is believed to be the earliest form of tennis. The game we observed was played within three walls of the cloisters using a gloved hand, propelling a hard bound leather ball off the walls and vigorously to each other. We were told that "tenez" was shouted to start the ball in play and in these early games the term "tenez" was used also to warn opponents to get ready to "receive it". Accordingly, the game soon became so popular that it provoked a trend to build new monasteries with places to play the game. Soon royalty started playing and adapting the game. Many French and English nobles spent so much time playing tennis and handball games that they neglected their duties as knights in favor of long hours on the courts.

As these medieval games developed out of the monasteries, others introduced racquets, nets, better balls, and a system for keeping score. Henry V111 was a most avid player of what became 'Royal Tennis'. He built a fine indoor court at his palace, Hampton Court, and played every day with his favored professional partners, always with sizeable wagers on the outcome. Many royals accumulated huge gambling debts, betting on and playing tennis. As the game became popular in the streets, gambling on matches and the large crowds generated became such a problem that it was banned for a time. It was not hard to believe that this simple game played in these medieval cloisters would become the forerunner, 500 years later, of our modern games of tennis, handball, bocce, racquetball, and squash.

After our tour of the Duomo, Mirium had lots of questions for our guide, Andre. He spoke fluent French and German, common in the border towns and villages of Northern Italy, along with some English to accommodate the tourists from America. We decided to take him for a late lunch. He borrowed a car from a friend and drove us a few miles out of town up into the mountain slopes. The views were spectacular. We soon arrived at a small, picturesque village, with only one place to eat. The only patrons there were local villagers who all seemed to know Andre well. Everyone spoke French. Several large delivery trucks dominated the parking lot and beyond.

There was no menu. The aroma of fresh herbs and roasted meats tantalized our eager tastebuds. Andre said that they serve only what is fresh on the day and for the season. All their herbs and vegetables were grown out back by the owners. It was 'prix fixe', in other words, one fixed price for lunch. We had a choice of four hors d'oeuvres. We decided to share the marinated wild mushrooms, and the sliced local veal sausage with marinated tomatoes. Accompanying this were thick slices of French peasant bread, with homemade duck pâté, fresh butter, and local olives. We were already quite full and opted to split the small pink crusted lamb chops with garlic, young white asparagus and of course very crispy pomme frites. No wonder all the truck drivers came many miles out of their way here for their lunch. The local house wine was a Trentino wine made from Moscato Gialto grapes and served liberally - all for one low price!

All through lunch, Andre enjoyed answering Mirium's questions about Medieval and Renaissance art. He proudly explained the main differences is that Renaissance Art used perspective, proper proportions, volume and light whereas with Medieval Art, the paintings were flat, did not have realistic proportions and used mostly single colours on objects. He explained that the Medieval Art in the Duomo was mostly depicting Christian subject matter, had elaborate decoration, bright colours, stylized figures and patterns and sometimes used gold, precious metals and gems, often denoting social status. The

Medieval Art sculpture and statues on pulpits and in chapels often were stiff and did not appear to have much depth, volume, or motion. This was evident in the Bolzano Duomo Cathedral chapel which was the first part and earliest of its construction. Andre then said the examples of Renaissance Art, such as the frescoes in the later construction of the cathedral proper showed more attention to proportions and detail as does Michelangelo's ceiling in the Sistine Chapel at the Vatican in Rome. His attention to detail, the showing of emotion on faces and of arms, hands and fingers are good examples of his more developed style, showing off his mastered skills with the use of depth and bright colours.

Other spots we hoped to visit included a much older medieval Castel Roncolo (known to the Germans as Schloss Runkelstein, meaning Runkelstein Castle) which was famous for the beer and cheese made by the monks at the monastery. There was also the 5000 yr. old Tyrolian hunter at the Tyrol Museum of Archaeology. Plus, we didn't want to forget the handwritten map our friend on the train had given us either. So much to do and so little time. We decided we should come back on our return trip to see it all. We only had through this evening to enjoy all the rich history this little town had to offer, as Mirium had managed to arrange an appointment in Venice on Friday morning with a fine art dealer.

We had already checked out of the hotel, which we had paid another day for to allow us to maximize our time without worrying about our luggage. The hotel was taking care of getting our bags taken to the train station for our 5:31 departure for Venice.

Since we still had time before our train, but not enough to do a formal tour, we pulled out the paper our friend from the train gave us to take a walk to the vista point. It seemed to be a part of town off the beaten path. That is usually the kind of place we like to explore, more of an adventure than a tourist destination.

The street was narrow with scaffolding up against one side. Apparently a bit of restoration work on the building façade, a very common site in all of Italy. There was a car parked at the other end, but we would still be able to walk around it. As we walked under the scaffolding, we commented on the fact that even though this was a workday, there were no workers in the area. A memory of O'Neil telling me to stay out of deserted alleys popped into my head. But that was London, this was Italy. The only other person we saw was a man getting into the car at the end of the road. As the car pulled away, there was a loud groaning of the scaffolding. It almost looked like the car was pulling the scaffolding behind it. Suddenly, the entire structure began crashing down around us. I grabbed Mirium and pushed her to the ground at the base of the wall, throwing myself over her to protect her from the falling scaffolding pieces. In a matter of seconds, the entire wall of scaffolding was on the ground, around us. By no small miracle, a sheet of plywood had wedged itself over us, protecting us from harm.

As we climbed our way out of the rubble, in total disbelief that we were not harmed, we looked around and saw no sign of the car at the end of the alley. For that matter, there was no sign of anyone. Apparently this alley was far enough off the beaten path that no one had heard the racket from the scaffolding collapsing. Once we were on solid footing, we looked at each other and Mirium threw herself into my arms, sobbing and shaking. "Thank God you weren't hurt! You could have been killed protecting me like that. You risked your life to keep me safe! I will never, ever forget this day! Or stop loving you!

We returned the way we had come, with so many unanswered questions. Was this just a freak accident? Was it planned? If so, then by whom? Was someone trying to scare us, or kill us? Should we report it to the authorities or should we be quiet and just get on the train and leave. We made our way to the train station, expecting at any moment for the police to come speeding around a corner in our direction. We looked a bit disheveled when we did pass an officer on the street in front of the station, but apparently not enough for him to question us.

Mirium went to the bank of payphones to confirm our hotels in Verona and Venice and our appointment on Friday, as I took a seat on one of the benches. I chose a location where I could keep an eye on her while scanning the people in the station for any signs of danger. She found a vacant phone between two other passengers. She couldn't help but notice the elderly lady decked to the nines, having an agitated conversation, at the phone to her left. She had apparently missed her train and was trying to get whoever was on the other end of the line to sort everything out. She wished she had time to help her, she looked so lost and confused.

The man on the phone to her right had his back toward her and looked like the average traveler. As she began dialing, she heard the man to her right laughing in what struck her as a somewhat evil sounding guffaw. His statement that followed made her blood run cold. "Tell the boss, it's all taken care of. Nobody could have survived that wreckage. When she doesn't show up, he'll be able to recover that painting without any interference from her or that boyfriend of hers, and no one will be the wiser. I'm grabbing a train down to Rome. I'll see you there."

Mirium turned her back to the man and slouched so he wouldn't notice her as he left. He hung up and headed in another direction to catch his train. She forgot about her calls and almost ran back to me. She relayed his conversation to me. I sat in silence for a bit, thinking. I suggested that she call her bank quickly before they close to get a status on her paintings.

This time we both went to the phone. When she identified herself to the receptionist that answered the phone, she said there was an urgency in the voice as she was asked to hold the line. The manager picked up the phone almost immediately, "Ms. Chamberlain, we have been trying to reach you since yesterday! I'm afraid we have some very troubling news. The move of your artwork was early yesterday morning. There was an armed robbery of the truck. And some of your paintings were among the ones stolen."

Mirium's face paled, as she almost dropped to the floor. I caught her as her knees buckled and the phone fell from her hand. I steadied her and she gave a weak nod that she was OK, and I picked up the phone to get the details from the manager on what caused her collapse. He kept saying "This has never happened before" as if he couldn't believe it was true. A thought flashed through my mind and before I hung up, I asked that he not tell anyone yet that he spoke with us. It was important that everyone think that no one had heard from us yet. Also pass that on to the receptionist who answered the phone. Hopefully she hadn't said anything yet. We didn't know who we could trust. I was left speechless as I hung up the receiver and helped Mirium to a bench.

16

Let's Get the Facts

The bank manager, Andrew Fredericks, was personally going to meet us the next day in Venice. We needed to call in the morning to make arrangements for a meeting. He gave us his personal number, so we could contact him at home before work. London was an hour behind us, so that would not be difficult. They were announcing the boarding for our train. We slowly made our way onto the track, up the steps and into some seats in the corner of the dining car. We were moving like two people in a trance. We were getting some strange looks from the other passengers. One older woman asked with a motherly voice, "Are you two alright?" I looked up at her and said, "Thank you, but we'll be fine." At this point, that last thing I was going to do was strike up a conversation with any more seemingly helpful strangers. I took Mirium's hands in mine across the table and gazed into her eyes. I had never seen her looking so lost and unnerved. My heart was breaking. All I could do was whisper, "Everything will be alright. We'll sort this out."

We used the lavatories on the train to clean up a bit and all-in-all looked like normal tired tourists when we finally settled back into our seats. Mirium, always serene and collected in a crisis, was quite nervous and edgy, said "I just want to be done with this business, find the painting, and get back home to Winston Gardens". Our train took us through Verona to continue east to the north coast of the Adriatic Sea and our destination in Venice.

I felt like I was in a nightmare that I couldn't seem to wake up from. I had moved to sit next to her, and she laid her head on my shoulder. As she drifted off to sleep, my mind was spinning with thoughts. At least we now knew why someone had been trying to kill us. But the overheard phone call left so many questions. As it occurred to me that we could move along for the rest of our trip in relative safety, since the one who apparently wanted us out of the way thought we were dead. I made a mental note that we shouldn't check in to our planned hotel in case there was someone there who would be watching for us. We needed to play along with the idea that we were dead.

We both must have dozed off. Suddenly they were announcing our arrival at the station in Venice. It was too late to get a car, and we needed to find a place to stay. We looked through the brochures for hotels and made some calls until we found a room. We made arrangements to get our luggage to our hotel and hailed a cab. A twenty and a wink to the desk clerk got us into a room as Mr. & Mrs. Smith, I got Mirium up to the room and she laid on the bed, looking exhausted. I told her to rest, that I was going down to use a payphone to call Michael Ladden again and wait for our luggage to arrive. I quietly prayed that he would answer his phone this time. We desperately needed his help.

I ordered a vodka at the bar off of the lobby and took it over to the phones. I looked at it and said, "Thanks, Yuri. Now I'm drinking straight vodka." I thought I should call him tomorrow. I dialed Ladden's phone, quietly pleading with him to answer it. My prayers were answered on the second ring. "Where have you been?!" I sounded like an overbearing mother. "I'm sorry, I didn't mean to sound like that. The last two days have been hell and we desperately need your help. Someone's been trying to kill us and some of Mirium art treasures have been stolen, and I think some Italian government officials are involved…" "Whoa, slow down!" he interrupted. "You sound like a crazy man. Back up and start from the beginning." I took a deep breath, a stiff gulp of my drink, and told him everything that had happened since we left Lausanne. He strongly concurred with playing dead and said the off the grid ploy at the hotel was good thinking. He would catch the first flight out in the morning and meet up with us in Venice. In the meantime, we were to keep a low profile. "Not a problem" I said, "I think we'll just sleep until this is all over." It was the closest I could come to a joke. I hung up and finished my drink just as our luggage arrived. The bellhop helped me with the luggage, being very quiet so as not to wake Mirium, who was sound asleep. I had asked for a 6 am wakeup call. It took no time for me to also be asleep.

I awoke the next morning before the wakeup call. My mind was running in circles. Mirium was still asleep, so I quietly got dressed and went downstairs to get some coffee from the lobby and call Ladden. The caffeine helped my thoughts snap back on track. I got through to Ladden just as he was getting ready to leave for the airport. I confirmed our hotel information. The flight was about 2 hours, so we could expect to see him around 9:30. We needed to call the banker in Lausanne at 6:30 to get his flight information.

When I spoke to Andrew, he reported that the box truck that was used at the heist was found parked at a rail loading area last night, in Vevey, about 10 miles east of Lausanne. Empty. The truck had been swept clean, no plates, but they were waiting for the forensics report this morning. He was hoping to have it in hand when he met with us. We had planned on meeting at our hotel lobby. There were several private meeting rooms on a mezzanine overlooking the lobby where we could sit in private and discuss the details of the case.

I was glad to see Ladden when he arrived. Mirium had been up for an hour and was almost ready to go downstairs for some breakfast. Ladden and I went down and enjoyed some fresh brewed, American style coffee while we waited for her. We didn't want to discuss anything important until she had joined us.

Mirium sat down and ordered an Earl Grey tea and a ricotta-stuffed pastry. Ladden asked that we go over the last 4 days. in as much detail as possible. He occasionally jotted notes on a pad and made comments on the murder attempts. He was particularly interested in how quickly after the theft our lives became at risk. He pointed out that this was a very well planned and thought-out heist, meaning that someone who knew about the upcoming movement of the art was involved. Having all of the players in place to follow our movements and coerce us into place for the attempts on our lives took a massive network of criminal elements. The phone conversation that Mirium overheard would indicate that mastermind was someone in a position of authority, who could place themselves in a position to take possession of the van Gogh that Mirium had lost without anyone questioning their activity. Ladden felt it was imperative that we 'stay dead' to flush out the culprit. We had no idea who was to be trusted. After a long discussion about who we could and maybe couldn't trust, we came up with a plan on how to proceed. His first plan was to find out if the Police Chief here in Venice was trustworthy. He called the local chief and introduced himself. He explained that we were on Holiday and had just recently become engaged. The bank called Mirium's lawyer since they were unable to get in touch with her. He in turn had reached out to Ladden to follow up on the theft until Mirium could be reached. They had fully expected to hear from her by now. Michael told him we hadn't arrived in Venice yet, even though we were scheduled to be here yesterday. Everyone assumed that the young couple had decided to spend some quiet time together, away from the stress of the outside world. He would let him know when we did show up. He also told him that he would take care of rescheduling the meeting they had arranged with the Italian Fine Arts Retrieval Bureau for when we got to Rome if it became necessary due to our delay. After all, the police had more important things to do than schedule meetings. When Ladden got off the phone he told us that the chief appreciated him taking care of the scheduling, but he insisted that he would make a call to them "just to let them know there may be a delay". The question we had was is this just a cultural courtesy thing or was he really calling the director to let him know that it appeared that we were, indeed, dead, since we hadn't shown up, and no one had heard from us.

Ladden checked into another hotel down the road, so as to not draw attention to where we were staying. When Andrew arrived around 11:00 am, At Michael's suggestion, we directed him to Ladden's hotel in case anyone was following him to be sure we weren't present at the meeting. We were already at the hotel in a private meeting room, and not visible to the outside world. Michael had reminded us that we still couldn't be sure that Andrew wasn't involved somehow. We were more inclined to believe that he may have inadvertently mentioned the relocation of the artwork to someone whom he erroneously trusted.

We spent the next hour going over all of the facts and details of the heist, the value of the paintings and the options for recovering them and the progress made so far.

Andrew had brought the original inventory of Mirium's assets, marked to show what had been taken. Apparently the thieves had very specific targets in the shipment. Whoever pulled this off had inside knowledge of what was in that truck and knew exactly what pieces were the most valuable. This was most distressing for the bank since nothing like this has ever happened before. The 'good news' from this is that they found the inside accomplice and have put additional measures in place to be sure that this will not happen again. Unfortunately, the connection to the inside was a blind alley. None of the communication was traceable, no names, no faces. Payments to the accomplices were in cash. Even the cash had been in plastic bags which had been disposed of, so there was nothing to do forensics on.

The banker and Ladden both agreed that usually if the paintings aren't recovered in the first 48 hours there is little chance of recovery. They get painted over and moved several times. There is frequently a buyer in the wings waiting to take possession. The extreme value of the van Gogh may slow down that process a bit. It seemed that the thieves did not want to keep the paintings local any longer than they had to, so it was likely that the process of camouflaging was put off until they felt comfortable having the artwork in one place for a while.

Andrew also told us that the initial forensics report had come in. It was a real long shot, but there were traces of coloured aggregate on the floor of the cab of the truck, probably from the driver's shoes. There was some natural red marble, which may have come from the area around Verona as well as some pigmented stone. The police were checking into where these two items might be available. The rest of the cab had been wiped clean. Whoever did was careful not to leave fingerprints. The police were suspecting an international team of professionals pulled together for this specific job. It was much too daring and carefully planned for any local crooks. As we wrapped up the meeting, Andrew checked his messages and there was one there with an update on the stone fragments.

It seems that there is a local aggregate supplier right here in Venice who uses both natural red marble from an area just north of Verona and also provides highly pigmented aggregate for decorative paving work. Michael took the information and said he would head over to their office right away.

Mirium and I continued to chat with Andrew. We thought it would be a good idea to talk to some of the local art authorities, keeping to vague discussions about obscure art pieces and their worth. How crooks handle paintings. Maybe also throw in some 'joking' questions about how one would go about obtaining such pieces. We also discussed how to handle the disposition of the painting, assuming that it was recovered.

Andrew grabbed a cab back to the airport and Mirium and I headed to the Mestre district to talk to an art restorer that Andrew had told Michael about.

Mestre is a working-class bedroom community for workers in Venice. About a half hour bus ride from downtown. This is where the workers commute daily by bus or scooter to service the tourist economy of Venice proper. Michael suggested we join the local throng on the bus. "Safety in numbers", he said. This was a highlight of our trip where we crowded in with the 'real people' who made Venice a great destination, all happy and chattering and pleased to share their stories, show us family pictures, and give us directions to where we were going and what stop to get off the bus.

We found our way to the art dealer using Michael's directions. His shop, which included a small gallery, was down a dingy, dark alleyway. Once there we were surprised to see in the back a working art studio. The dealer showed us several works he was restoring. He said many of the art thieves 'paint over' expensive fine art to avoid detection. He showed us an old Le Trek he was restoring by removing the overpaint very carefully so as to clean and restore it to its former brilliance. He said this was a work commissioned by Italy's National Archives. It had recently been recovered in a police raid in Milan after having disappeared for forty years. The restored colours of the part of the painting that was visible were textured and brilliant. This restoration was painstaking work. He advised us also to visit 'the bureau' in Rome. He was going to give us a letter of introduction to Capt. Alberto Giovanni, but we told him we would prefer it if he didn't mention our visit to anyone. We simply explained that there seemed to be a breach in security somewhere and we didn't know where yet. Best to keep our moves quiet. We headed back to our hotel for a short rest.

Michael in the meantime had located the office of the stone company. He checked with the front desk clerk on how long a drive it was to that address. The clerk said It was about a 45-minute drive, so Michael rented a car. Said he would be back in time for dinner. Most of the drive was on a two-lane highway with lots of truck traffic. He was able to find the location with no trouble, thanks to the map the rental car company had given him. He was directed to the office by the gate keeper. He entered a smallish room with three men sitting at desks and having a good laugh about something in Italian. He nodded as he entered and asked, in what little Italian he knew, if anyone spoke English. One of the younger men said he spoke some. Michael explained as simply as he could why he was there.

"Yeah, we had a guy working for us for a couple of years, who suddenly quit last week. Said he had something in the works so he wouldn't have to work in this f-ing dust bowl any longer".

Michael asked for a name and address, and the English-speaking guy retold his story to someone who must have been the boss. He looked Michael over, thought a minute, then nodded to the kid who produced a pen and paper on which to write the information. He handed it to Michael, who very gratefully said "thank you" in Italian and headed back to Venice.

Ladden stopped at the first pay phone and called our hotel. We had just gotten to the room and were hoping to hear from him. He shared his success with us and said he was going to the address they gave him. We told him we were exhausted and were going to rest for a couple of hours.

Michael had a permit to carry throughout Europe and had brought his gun with him. It may come in handy encouraging information out of the suspect. He also called the local police to inform them of the situation and gave them the name and number of the police in Lausanne so they could verify his story. They requested that he not enter the property until their man was present. He'd play that by ear. As it turned out, the call to Lausanne prompted a full-blown team to show at the residence. They were experienced enough to arrive with no sirens. They surrounded the building the apartment was in, and Michael went to the front door and knocked. A tall, lanky, light-haired man answered the door, barely opening it, and said something in Italian. Michael shrugged and said "English?" At that point the man noticed the police car across the street and slammed the door to run. Michael kicked the door back open and followed, gun drawn. The man ran out his back door, only to find three cops with firearms pointed at him. Michael followed the cops to the police station. He had the feeling that this guy never had a gun pointed at him before. It made his situation come into clear focus and he couldn't wait to cooperate. Sadly, like the insider at the bank, he had very limited knowledge of what he was involved in. He drove a truck containing four masked men. He heard them speak some English, but mostly Italian. Left the first vehicle where the Lausanne police had found it and switched to a large van. At Milan he pulled into a gas station, took his payment which was cash in a plastic bag in the cab of the truck, walked the couple of blocks to the train station and boarded a train for home.

Michael was provided an interpreter to allowed him to interrogate the prisoner, with a local inspector present. The conversation was transcribed so they could fax it to the Police in Lausanne. Michael hit paydirt when the suspect remembered overhearing part of a conversation during which one of the men said, "We'll head south to Florence, then wait for our instructions." He was also able to give a description of the van they were driving, though he didn't notice the plates. The police put out an APB on a white, unmarked van, no windows past the first row and no markings. It would be too late to set up roadblocks, as the van was probably already in Florence by now. Of course, that description fit more vehicles than could be stopped, but they will be on the lookout for unusual activity or parking behavior for such a vehicle.

While he was out chasing the bad guy, we were feeling the effects of the adrenaline and stress of the last few days. We fell asleep as our heads touched the bed. When we woke the sun was already beginning its retreat towards the horizon. We could see the pigeons massing in the square below our window. We lay in bed, enjoying the subtle changes in the twilight coming in through our window. I lay on my side next to her. She rested her right hand on my hip, her left hand up above my head on my pillow. I could smell the wonderful faint scent from her body lotion. It was intoxicating. She nestled in closer, and we cuddled like two teddy bears. She shivered as I grazed her nipple with my cheek. Her nipples firmed and her body responded as I moved over her, my organ erect. She groaned softly, as I entered her. We took our time and relished every moment of being alive and together, our bodies in perfect synchrony. The protracted anticipation of climax kept building until we both cried out in total release. When we were able to move, we showered together and got ready to go out for the evening.

The phone rang and it was Ladden. He filled us in on his success with the arrest and interrogation. We were thrilled with this news. We didn't mention our afternoon activities.

17

Public Places

Ladden grabbed the first flight he could get to Florence. The plan was for Mirium and me to drive there and meet up with him the next day. Mirium had tickets to a fundraiser this evening. We thought the distraction would be a good break for our nerves and decided to attend.

It was a very well attended cocktail party at the Teatro La Fenice, the opera house of Venice, one of the oldest and most famous in Italian theatre. A four-piece ensemble played in the background as the champaign flowed and snappy waiters passed around hors d'oeuvres and canapes. Lots of old wrinkled tanned women with their portly husbands. A few very rich old men had their young trophy wives hanging off one arm. Formal dress, lots of jewelry and lots of chatter. A discrete jewel thief would have had a grand time. My new tux was perfectly suited for the occasion and of course Mirium looked stunning in her long silky white, backless gown with the classic slit up the side, showing off her never disappointing, long, slender yet shapely legs. The elegance of her look was completed by the simple, albeit expensive, diamonds. As people turned to look at her, I began to feel uneasy about being in such a public event.

This event was a fundraiser for the street children of Venice. I realized that as Mirium was a patron of one of London's orphanages a few people there might recognize her. We gazed at the grand frescoes and works of art around the large reception room. There was dancing and entertainment by the ensemble with

Italy's most famous opera singer who sang some numbers from the Opera opening the next week.

We had only been there about 10 minutes, trying to avoid direct contact with anyone, and on the lookout for anyone who might look familiar. Neither of us was really in the mood for mingling and idle conversation. We were slowly making our way towards the door to leave when we heard a woman next to us say "Oh, there's the Chief of Police. I was surprised he wasn't here this evening, with all of this wealth mulling about." We spun about to turn our backs to the door and made our way off to the side. Although we hadn't met, I suspect he had seen pictures of our faces. As he proceeded further into the room, we quickly made our way to the door and exited, confident that we had left undetected.

We left the event, planning on a brief walk before a late dinner. As we strolled along the canals the sun was beginning to set. We turned a corner, and the view made us stop in our tracks and stare in awe. The blue of the twilight sky was mirrored in the water of the canal before us. Turning it into a vivid azure colour. The lights of the city had turned on and were reflected as long streaks of gold in the reflection. Indeed, the entire scene along the waterfront had taken on a golden hue from the lights, the rooftops ending against a rose tone horizon that gradually blended into more subtle gold tones before fading into the blue above us. There was a solitary gondola in the canal, being skillfully guided, barely creating a ripple, with the low tones of the voice of the gondolier serenading his lovestruck passengers as they became an integral part of this romantic scene. After pausing long enough to turn and share our own embrace and kiss to complete the moment, we continued along our way, becoming part of the wonder that we had, moments before, only been observers of.

We walked across to the Casino where we had dinner reservations, at the Wagner, under the name of Smith. We were hoping that even though we had arrived early they would still be able to seat us. The restaurant, a tribute to Wagner, a classical composer and a longtime resident of Venice, was famous for its three special rooms adorned with different fine art paintings, frescoes and classical sculpture.

The maître d' greeted us. He was short, fat, and bald with bad teeth. He smelled of cheap hair tonic and swept what hair he had over his bald forehead. Why a restaurant of this caliber would have this man as the first encounter with guests, I couldn't fathom. There was a bit of a raised eyebrow at our name, which warranted a tip for discretion, and another for seating us both early and in an obscure location. My stomach was rumbling as the few snacks at the party made me even more hungry. The restaurant was full of rich people, some of whom had spilled over from the Opera reception. No one seemed to pay any special attention to the maître d', as if he fit in perfectly with the ambiance of the establishment. As a matter of fact, some of the patrons seemed to greet him with warmth and respect as if he were a long-time member of their family. I wished we had chosen a more off-the-beaten-path establishment in which to dine. We had a superbly prepared dinner of local seafood, followed by a fine steak with perfectly presented local vegetables. The desserts were spectacular. Mirium commented on how she loved watching me enjoy my meal. We were able to leave discreetly, mostly hidden from sight behind the many large plants located throughout the establishment. We grabbed a cab back to the hotel.

Back at our hotel, we had a discussion about how, in order to play dead, you really must stop living. We had been foolish going out this evening.

The drive to Florence would take about three hours, so before we left, we visited two of the many prominent art dealers, taking care not to mention anything about van Gogh. One was an art gallery, just off the square, which seemed to have a lot of memorabilia surrounding art deals of some of the great masters. We commented on them to the owner, and he was only too happy to elaborate on the deals, boasting that he had brokered some of the most expensive sales in the art world. He said he always had several possible buyers on call, ready to make offers on rare collectibles. "As everyone in the art world knows," he said, "previously unknown works by the great master's do occasionally pop up and the demand for these gems never diminishes. He pointed to one picture in particular and bragged that "this is one of me with the Director of 'the Bureau' in Rome!" We feigned ignorance and looked at him quizzically. "Of course! You would have no reason to know about 'the Bureau'. How silly of me. I am an old man who gets carried away with my talk." He went on to explain about the Fine Arts Retrieval Bureau, and how a connection to them was the envy of every art dealer. We showed the appropriate amount of awe and admiration to bolster his ego, but no more interest than an average affluent tourist would normally show. He looked around his empty shop as if to see if anyone was listening or could hear our conversation and motioned us closer as one would before telling a secret. We looked at each other, smiling as if this was a game and shrugged, as if to say we had no clue of what he was about to tell us, then we edged closer to listen. He said there were rumors that several pieces of priceless worth, had been stolen and that one of them was a Titian, which an investigator he was familiar with had recovered, just this morning, right here in Venice! We both listened and took a mental note of the investigator's name. There is supposed to be another unnamed piece which the Director of the Bureau himself will be acting as agent for the sale of if it is recovered. I made as if I were trying to stifle a yawn and Sr. Castiglio, apologized with all sorts of body language and words, for going on so long that he wore us out. In a final habitual motion, he handed us his business card and offered some suggestions for dinner. We explained that were heading out of town that afternoon.

18

Yuri's Help

We had driven for a little over two hours and were getting hungry. We skipped breakfast so we could visit the art dealers. We got off the highway at Rioveggio and followed the sign to the right at the end of the ramp. We made a left at the main road and saw a restaurant on our left. It looked closed, so we continued on the road, since it was heading in the right direction for Florence. We had thought it might be nice to actually try pizza for lunch, since neither of us had ever had pizza in Italy. We drove on for about 5 or 6 miles and spotted a pizzeria on the left in Dal Tosco. It had a couple of tables outside and we took a seat. A waitress came out and Mirium conversed with her in Italian. As we waited for our tomato, basil and feta pizza to come out, a couple of workers from the construction across the street started singing at the street corner right in front of us, they were joined by two others, then four more came up from the other direction. Before we knew it, there must have been sixteen men singing what Mirium said was an Italian folk ballad. It appeared we were in for a local tradition and an unforgettable treat. We found out from our waiter that this happens most days in the summer. The men all worked in the area and came there to sing in their lunch hour. They were waiters, lawyers, shopkeepers, accountants, chefs, delivery drivers. Men from all walks of life just coming together to sing. We were so lucky to have picked this particular restaurant to enjoy our lunch.

Before we returned to the highway to continue to Florence, we stopped at a petrol station to make some calls. Mirium called Andrew Fredericks at the bank to see if he had any news and update him on what our plans were. He had, of course heard of the

Titian being recovered. We told him about the information Ladden had gotten from the truck driver and that Ladden was in Florence, and we were less than an hour from there. Andrew was certain that if they had headed as far as Florence, then they would be going to Rome. After she recounted the comments by the gallery owner, and considering the phone conversation that Mirium had overheard, he admitted that it was looking like someone high up in The Bureau might be involved in all of this. That would also explain why the paintings had made their way to Italy, rather than just remain in Switzerland. After she finished the call and filled me in, I called the hotel where Michael said he would be staying. They rang me through to his room, but there was no answer. I left a message that we would be in Florence in an hour and would wait for him at the public library, within view of the main entrance. We got the number for the library and called for directions. We were eager to meet up with Ladden and compare notes. As soon as we got back on the highway, we entered a 6-mile-long tunnel, one of the many tunnels along the route through central Italy. Mirium commented that she was glad people thought we were dead, otherwise these tunnels would be a very fearful place.

As we drove through the local streets in Florence we noticed a Russian speaking neighborhood. I decided to give Yuri a call and let him know what was going on. It was unlikely that he would have any contacts in Italy, but it was worth a try. I used a payphone outside of the library. He sounded eager to help. He didn't like the idea that someone was trying to kill his nephew's trainer. He said he had a cousin in Florence and asked if we were anywhere near there. I laughed and said "Standing in the middle of Florence right now. This was where the last lead told us the painting was heading. Just waiting to meet up with Michael Ladden. He's been working the case." Yuri asked where we were and said his cousin would meet us there. He could only speak some English but spoke fluent Italian. As I concluded the conversation with Yuri, Michael came walking around the corner towards us. He said his car was parked about two blocks away at a parking garage. He told us he had met with the local police this morning and had given them a description of the van. They contacted the Milan authorities and got a list of stolen or missing vans from the last week. They put out a bulletin with likely matching models and plates and about a half hour ago they got a hit on a van in a parking garage near here. That's where he parked. As we spoke, a black sedan pulled up along the curb. A medium height wall of muscle got out of the driver's seat and approached us. "Jack Hardigan?" I nodded, feeling a bit intimidated. "I'm Ivan Sacca, Yuri's cousin," he said in broken English. I turned to Mirium and asked, "Can you do the introductions in Italian? Please." She smiled, glad to be needed, and introduced herself, Michael and me. They exchanged pleasantries and she asked us what we wanted to tell him. Michael said "Tell him we found a van in a parking lot close by and were just going over to look at it. Would he join us?" Mirium translated and Ivan gave a short "Da". As we approached the lot, Ivan started speaking in Italian to Mirium. She translated, telling us that he knows the attendant there. It's his wife's brother-in-law, Danil.

After Ivan and Danil greeted each other in Russian, we were shown the location of the van. Mirium asked Ivan if Danil had seen anyone or anything around this van or it's movements. The van was parked out of his sight, but there was a black minivan that had come and gone within maybe 20 minutes, paid cash. He did mention that they had security cameras that may have picked up that location. Just about that time, the police inspector showed up and Mirium filled him in. We went into the office to view the security tapes. The security cameras panned the area, and the criminals were very careful to stay out of sight when the camera was pointing toward the van. There was one scene which we went back to look at. where we thought we could see the corner of a picture frame in the back of the black minivan. The license plate had been covered with tape, but the left rear fender had a small dent in it where someone must have bumped into it in a parking lot. The police took the tape back to their office to have someone freeze pictures of the van and the damaged bumper for distribution. I was walking around the garage, absent mindedly looking for any clues. My eye fell on a reflection in a mirror mounted at the exit, of a car pulling out. I had a clear view of the front license plate! I turned and frantically looked for the nearest camera that might catch the mirror in its scan. "There!" I shouted. Michael and Danil came running over. "We need the tape from that camera." Michael looked around and saw the mirror. "Nice work, Jack!" Danil caught on to what we were looking at and ran to put the tape in his machine. He rewound to the approximate time and within a few seconds, we had the license plate number of the minivan. It had the unmistakable 'Roma' for the province code.

Michael took the information to the police station and picked up a copy of the van picture. He would get the information on the registration and formulate the next move. In the meantime, Mirium and I were to head to Rome and hold up for the night.

A quick call got us two rooms in downtown Rome. Once we had the name and address of the hotel, we called Ladden at the police station and gave him the information. We got back on the road and headed to Rome. We had a three-hour drive ahead of us.

.

19

Rome

We arrived in Rome just as the night crowd was beginning to take over the streets. This type of driving was more stressful than we needed after an exhausting day. We were relieved to finally pull up in front of the hotel and hand the keys to the valet and let the bell hop handle our bags. We checked in and Mirium asked the desk clerk for a recommendation for a quick and quiet dinner. She suggested that the room service from the hotel might be our best option on a Saturday evening. She assured us that the food was "deliziosa".

The bell hop led the way up to our suite and as he closed the door behind him it felt like we had just been closed off from the rest of the world. The furnishings and colours were calming, the quiet was serene. Our view from our window overlooked an area filled with rooftop gardens, with lights that were just beginning to twinkle in the twilight. I reached for her hand and pulled her close to me. We stood there for a long moment embracing each other, feeling the warmth of each other's skin, taking comfort is each other's scent and forgetting the craziness of the world out there. We relaxed our pose, sighing deeply, and turned to the task of unpacking and ordering dinner. We joked that we were so exhausted, that these tasks were almost more than we could muster the energy for. Turns out the desk clerk was not exaggerating about the food, and it was definitely worth the effort. It was, however, the last thing that we had energy for, and we were soon curled up in each other's arms, fast asleep.

The next morning was Sunday and there was no reason for us to wake up early. I am sure that there were Church bells ringing in our neighborhood, but we never heard them.

We eventually got up and went out to join the rest of the world. The pigeons were there as always on the steps of the local church, below the Spanish steps. These steps have been written about for centuries and have been a meeting place for poets, writers and painters for many years. Now tourists are there en masse in the summer, taking pictures on their way to the Trevi Fountain not far from the lower level, and the many coffee shops and boutiques nearby. The unique design and elegance of the steps have made this spot a favorite meeting place for both tourists and locals alike.

It was one of those mornings to linger over a cappuccino and pastry. The Borghese Gardens were a couple of blocks away. We walked the half mile to a little Café located one block off of the Gardens, away from the rush and bustle of the traffic horns and weaving motor scooters. It was a good opportunity to collect our thoughts.

Mirium blew on the foam on top of her cappuccino as we relaxed in the Borghese coffee shop. "Do you remember the Sicilian man we met at the Opera fundraiser", "yes, his eyes were all over me." "He may be useful in our search if it appears the Sicilian mob may have taken the paintings". We decided to now take in the rest of the museum. From the gardens of the Borghese, it was about a mile walk down the hill to the Pantheon, the best preserved of all the Roman sights. The temple, started in 609BC, replaced an earlier temple during the reign of Augusta. Rebuilt by Hadrian and completed in 126AD. It is famous for its brick dome and is considered an architectural wonder of the ancient world. We marveled at the tall marble columns and of course the huge domed ceiling. All the huge bronze side doors were open today and a light summer breeze blew over us as we imagined ourselves being in ancient Rome.

Next to the huge side doors there were large full length lace curtains blowing in the breeze. We happened to be there just as a modern dance practice was beginning. All barefoot women flitting around on the mosaic grey marble floor to the music of a muted flute and lyre. They were rehearsing for a movie scene to be shot in the building the next day. At least we hadn't lost our luck of being in the right place at the right time to enjoy wonderful moments in life.

Michael had called the Bureau first thing in the morning to get an appointment with the director. The earliest he could meet would be after lunch. Michael didn't mention that he would not be alone.

We were to meet with Capt. Alberto Giovanni. His office was on the fifth floor of an old grey building housing the Italian Police in central Rome. The old elevator creaked as we took it up to the fifth floor.

Michael pressed the buzzer. The door opened by itself like the door of a safe. We stepped in and paused. The seating area reminded me of that of an airport lounge with dark green furniture. His outer office had several expensive looking Turkish carpets spread on a dark hardwood floor. A lone fan whirled slowly and silently in the centre of the ceiling and there was a large plasma screen at one end. Being summer, all the windows were open wide filling the room with the horns and hum of the traffic five floors below. Those Italians loved to drive fast with horns blaring!

The receptionist was an elderly lady who fit in perfectly with the ancient city around her. She checked Michael's name against the appointment book on her desk and asked him to have a seat and she would let the Director know he was here. She glanced in our direction with mild interest.

As Michael sat down next to us, she picked up her phone and announced Michael's arrival. She casually mentioned that it was Michael and two guests. She probably had judged from Mirium's appearance that she was a woman of stature, and asked if she would like some tea. Mirium politely declined.

The man we were waiting to meet with was the longtime Director of The Italian Fine Arts Recovery Bureau, judging by a photograph on the wall of him standing with the current Pope, he was a tall greying man with a bushy moustache. Looked as though he might be close to retiring from the position. While we were waiting, two other men entered and approached the receptionist. The older of the two introduced the younger man. I did not catch the name, but my ears perked up when I heard him say that he was to be the new director when Capt. Giovani retired later this year. The Bureau had been established after the Second World War, tasked with the recovery of lost or stolen art in Europe. The Nazis had taken possession of much of Europe's fine art. It had been hidden away, only to be lost, forgotten or some even hidden in other countries, many as far away as South America.

The receptionist answered her phone, then came over to us and said the Director was ready for us. She ushered us over to the double doors to his office and opened them for us to enter, closing them behind us. The captain was engrossed in a paper on his desk and didn't look up immediately. Michael was standing between his desk and us and softly cleared his throat. As Captain Giovanni looked up from his papers, Mirium and I moved next to Michael, into clear view. The colour momentarily drained from the captain's face as he began, "I thou...".

Michael had turned toward us to make the introductions, pretending not to notice the obvious surprise on the part of the captain, as he recognized who we were. It only took him a second to regain his composure an offer his hand to us in greeting. It is a pleasure to finally meet you. Ms. Chamberlain, I am so sorry that you have had to suffer this distress at the loss of your artwork. I assure you we are doing everything we can to track down the paintings."

Capt. Giovanni spoke very good English. He had a large red face with tufts of stubble protruding from a puffy chin. There was a large lump over his left eye, which moved up and down when he got excited or laughed. It was difficult not to stare at it. After introductions he said that the bureau had been successfully recovering fine art for many years. He said in the last two years they had recovered over two hundred art pieces, arresting many of the criminals, finding long lost artworks, resulting in welcome fees and revenue for the Italian Government. He brought the conversation around to the theft of our van Gogh, sounding somewhat apologetic, as if he felt somehow personally responsible for the theft of our property in his country. "Usually" he said, "the front page in Rome was devoted to the fortunes of football teams, the exaggerated promises of politicians, or the latest on the war between local fishermen and environmentalists". However, this day was devoted to accounts of several thefts of fine art. One account described how an expensive sculpture was smuggled out of the national museum in a beer barrel from their cafe, and another of a 15th century painting that was stolen from under the nose of a local collector. What was of note was that the painting had been immediately concealed by painting over the original with a much lesser work. The robbery in Lausanne was also mentioned in the article, listing the three paintings that were taken along with their estimated value.

Mirium produced the letter of introduction from her bank, along with the original bill of sale for her Van Gogh, papers of authenticity from the bank, her insurance papers, and a photograph of the work. He said, "As I told Mr. Ladden over the phone, he had several detectives assigned to the case and his office was spreading the word. He personally had met with the detective investigating the robbery in Lausanne. All this had resulted in the recovery of the Titian, in Venice, which had also been painted over to hide it. They were now on the trail of the Caravaggio and our Van Gogh but did not have much to go on. From their sources in Venice, they only knew that the other two paintings did not appear to still be in Venice. The thieves were smart enough to separate the artwork to make it more difficult to track it down. We had already planned on keeping the information we had learned in Florence to ourselves for the moment. Michael was not inclined to trust the Director. We gave him our contact information and we said we would be staying in Rome for another week. Michael, we said, would be staying on the trail of the painting as long as it took to recover it. The Director assured us that he would keep us informed as any information came to light. He also gave us some suggestions of sights we might enjoy that wouldn't be overly crowded.

We left the office and Michael said he was going to stop in at the police downstairs and see what he could learn. In the meantime, he suggested that we enjoy the city, just keeping to crowded areas where we had safety in numbers, staying close to each other, and being very vigilant and aware of our surroundings. I told him that staying close was the easy one, as I smiled and pulled Mirium closer to my side. He mentioned that it was unlikely that anyone would make another attempt on our lives this 'close to home', but one can never be too sure. It was obvious that our appearance had rattled the Director, and desperation can cause stupid moves.

Our hotel in central Rome was only a 3 star but well maintained, clean and comfortable. The main attraction for me was that our room was a large suite, which had a huge Roman style bath right in the corner of our spacious living room, perfect for a long, sensuous soak together after a long day of sightseeing, ancient ruins and art galleries. It was one of those big old brown, earthenware tubs that you could disappear below the edge of when sitting in it. It must have been fifty years old. Less than a block from our hotel, the white Spanish Steps climb a steep slope between Piazza di Spagna at the base, to Piazza Trinta del Monti at the top.

We knew that Rome traffic congestion was legendary. However, we could walk to almost everywhere we wished to go from our hotel. It was an unusually grey day for Rome with some light drizzle. Outside on the streets, all the people and traffic were in frantic blurred motion. We were advised by Capt. Giovanni to go to the Borghese Gallery and Gardens as they currently had an exhibit of Cezanne and Van Gogh's works, many from private collections, rarely seen in a public exhibit before. We took a short cab ride, with our driver pointing out the Seven Hills of Rome which were mostly untouched by the great fire during Nero's time as emperor. The Borghese Gallery, located in the original Borghese family mansion housed one of the great collections of fine Italian art. There were Roman sculptures and mosaics, the old masters including Raphael, Titian, Michelangelo, and Caravaggio. We went straight to the Cezanne, Van Gogh exhibit. We bought the exhibit book and sat down to wait. We had an appointment with the curator of the exhibit but were a little early. We were astounded at how prolific Van Gogh was during his lifetime, especially when he lived in Arles on the French coast. This was when he lived with Paul Gauguin and the infamous incident occurred when Vincent cut off his left ear while in one of his temper outbursts.

The curator came out to greet us, very enthusiastically. He said Capt. Giovanni had called and he knew about our search and would be glad to help us find our Van Gogh.

He was passionate about the artist! He said Vincent was very prolific, painting every day, only pausing to eat and drink wine, relying on his brother to support him. He said that over a ten-year period he produced 1,200 works that he knows of, including 860 oils, some drawings, mostly landscapes and portraits. His most famous works, such as 'The Almond Blossoms', 'The Potato Eaters', 'The Sunflowers' collection, and 'The Starry Night' are now worth millions. He died with little recognition, still very poor.

We interrupted his lecture on van Gogh, "We'd love to learn more about the artist, but can you tell us anything about the stolen art?" "Oh, yes, sorry! I just love the story behind the works, and can't help myself, but talk about it." he answered. He said he knew about the bank theft in Lausanne and of the recovery of the Titian. The Titian was now worth 10 million USD! He also said that the chances of recovery were pretty good since the bureau had recovered one of the stolen treasures already. He also passed on his own thought, that it could have been the Milan mafia who had stolen the paintings.

He asked if we had any ideas who might have masterminded such a daring heist. Any clues? We feared he was fishing for information to feed back to the Director, so we sadly denied knowing anything more than the Director had told us. We added, "Everything seems to lead to dead ends. We can only hope that the authorities here in Rome find something before it is too late to recover the paintings, and we need to give up."

He encouraged us to have faith, and let the professionals do their job. He offered any help we thought he might be able to give and told us to let him know if we find anything out that he may be able to help with.

We took our taxi back to our hotel and took a late afternoon siesta and bath. Our hotel front desk suggested several restaurants within walking distance. We decided on Trattoria Monti, a family run traditional Italian restaurant serving organic fruits and vegetables, fresh fish and meats from central Italy. This restaurant was famous for its ancient Roman wall which is still intact within its rooms. Our table was located next to the ancient red brick wall. We had the antipasto to start, then I ordered the grilled fish, Mirium, the veal with herbs. We both had their perfectly cooked risotto with wild mushrooms, ending a wonderful meal with their fresh raspberries and cream.

We walked back passing the Trevi Fountain, which was lit up, showing off its exquisite baroque figures. Trevi means three streets and was a water source for central Rome. Legend says that 'If you throw a coin in the fountain with your right hand over your left shoulder you will return to Rome someday'. Mirium and I hoped we would be back.

Now that we were alive again, a tour seemed the best way for us to use our time to see some of Rome, while staying in public places with lots of people. The next morning, we went on a tour of the Forum and the Colosseum. The Roman Forum, originally a marketplace in ancient Rome and the scene of public meetings and law courts. The Colosseum was the largest building in Rome and one of the new seven wonders of the world. It is over 1900 years old and dominates the area. The huge oval stone structure was the site of thousands of gladiatorial contests against multiple wild beasts where trained gladiators fought each other to the death. Our guide said that over twelve thousand gladiators had died during this period. Much of the ancient city was severely damaged and the Colosseum closed after an earthquake in 1349. Being around crowds of manic tourists, visiting the historic sites, all that excitement eventually seeps into your bones. At the Colosseum our guide had a pass to take us to the restricted lower level. This is where all the stadium killing shows were staged from. The gladiators and wild animals were winched up to the stadium floor on mechanical platforms and lifts. It opened up into a huge area where wild tigers, giraffes, lions and crocodiles could be held, then raised up for the gladiators to stage contests for the great amusement of the large bloodthirsty crowds. Our guide said that at one time the stadium floor could be flooded to have fights with elephants and alligators with gladiators on boats or rafts. What a show it must have been!

We made our way back through the Forum. It was only midafternoon but dark clouds were gathering. We took a short detour through the ancient ruins, ending up in the Museum of Ancient Roman Archaeology before the afternoon storm hit. We wandered through rooms of statuary and examples of Roman art which included architecture, painting, sculpture and mosaic work, ancient luxury objects in metalwork, gem engraving, ivory carvings, glass work, and frescoes. We saw floor and wall mosaics depicting ancient Roman life made from hundreds of small coloured tiles which came from excavations of public buildings and houses of the wealthy, restored for display. Mirium enjoyed the exhibits, while I pretended to be riveted by the experience, while I was actually focused on keeping lookout for anything suspicious.

After the storm had cleared and the sun began to set, I was getting hungry and ready for some classic Roman food I had had my fill of milling around with other tourists. I don't mind being part of the tourist groups in short spurts; however, I really do enjoy the tranquility of a great meal or lingering quiet time with Mirium, or just being by myself after all of the high spirits of the other tourists. It was nice then to just retreat to a quiet cafe or go back to the tranquility of our room.

We were walking towards Piazza di Spagna after an exhausting day. As usual, we could see lots of tourists milling around the Spanish Steps. We turned the corner towards the steps behind our hotel, next to the underground parking garage, happily chatting about our dinner plans, Among the many cars going in and out of the garage, I vaguely noticed a dark green van pull up beside us. After returning to the states last year, I grew out of the habit of constantly looking over my shoulder since spending the winter in Eugene, Oregon, which isn't exactly a hot spot of criminal activity. Some small part of my mind took note of the van and a man opening the side door, but I didn't react quickly enough. Two husky, brutes jumped out of the van and a third came up behind me, breathing heavily down my neck and pushing a gun barrel in my back. I raised my arms for all to see, maybe at least one of the many onlookers would understand the action and help or call for police. I turned enough to see my assailant just as I saw the other two men grab Mirium and lift her. I took my chances, and just as he was trying to slam the butt of the gun into my head, I moved enough to make it a glancing blow and managed to trip him, punched him hard on the jaw, then pounced on top of him as he fell. I forced his nose into the pavement and grabbed his gun. As this was happening, I had been able to make out the other two who were forcing a kicking and screaming Mirium, into the sliding side door. The two jumped in after her and slammed the door, as the van was pulling away. That was all I remember. It was as if time stood still. I may never forget the sound of her cries for help. It all happened in a matter of seconds, and she was gone. As the tourists around me broke free from their wide-eyed disbelief and processed what they had just seen, someone stepped forward and took the gun from my hand. I heard him say he was a cop, then everything began spinning as I rolled over onto my back. The noise became deafening, the din from the crowd, people shouting in Italian. I could make out words like "polizia" and "ambulanza", Over all of this was the approaching sirens of police or maybe ambulance or both, and someone who just kept shouting at me "Stai bene? Stai bene?" alternating with broken English "Are you alright?" All I wanted to do was chase after that van, but when I tried to get up, my head spun wildly, making me nauseous, with a splitting headache. I reached up to place my hand on the area that hurt and discovered a good size bump where my assailant had managed to connect with my head. I slumped back against a good Samaritan who was helping to support me as I sat on the ground. There was a commotion in the crowd as a uniformed police officer made way for the ambulance crew to get to me. The plain clothed policeman who had taken the gun cuffed the man I had overtaken. As they led him to a car, I desperately wanted to follow and question him. Who were they? Where had they taken Mirium? Why did they do this? Neither the police nor the medical team would allow that.

The technicians were thorough and pleasant. They spoke English; a necessity in a city heavily visited by American tourists. I said repeatedly that I was fine, just wanted to get back to my hotel and start looking for my Mirium. They were having nothing to do with that idea until they were sure that I was uninjured. I was checked for broken bones, neurological damage, and of course, a concussion. They placed an ice pack on the bump on the back of my head and bandaged a scrape I got when I fell to the ground, just as the police approached with their questions. I was still a bit foggy and irrational, as I kept insisting to the police that I just needed to leave and find Mirium. They also would have nothing to do with that plan and in retrospect, I'm surprised they didn't restrain me to stop me from running off. Once the ambulance crew gave me a clean bill of health and left me with instructions, the police took me by the arm and asked where I was staying. When they discovered it was so close by, they suggested that we relocate to the hotel for questions in a more private and controlled setting.

The manager came straight out when he saw us enter and ushered us to his private office. An older balding man with a slight tick in his left eye. He looked down, glasses lowered, pinched the bridge of his nose, paused, then said, in his heavily accented English, "my apologies for your grief at this moment" and "we will do everything we can to recover your Mirium, our valued guest". He said that these kidnappings are becoming a daily occurrence in Rome and will become a severe blight on the tourist industry. Usually, it was children that were taken. Now, many parents are having their children escorted to school and returned with security men as a precaution against kidnapping. I didn't say anything, but I didn't think this was a random kidnapping. I was sure it had to do with our pursuit of the stolen van Gogh.

The police detective seemed to know what he was doing and took the questions slowly and deliberately. He said he had a good chance to find where Mirium might be held if he can pressure the man I had captured. He said that from my descriptions of the men in the van he had a pretty good idea which gang had done the kidnapping but made no promises or predictions.

I told him everything I could remember, then filled him in on the missing van Gogh and gave him the name of the police detective working on the case. I also asked them to get in touch with Michael Ladden, as he was working the case for us.

He agreed that this might not be typical ransom kidnapping but asked that I not answer the room phone until he could have his men tap our line.

I finally got back to the room. From there I called Yuri. He was out but his secretary said he would call me back. I was talking to O'Neill back in London when there was a knock at the door. It was the hotel security manager and the police detective with an additional officer who went about setting up the wiretap and planting cameras and bugs in the room. The detective asked if there was anything else that I had remembered or wanted to tell him. I decided I trusted him enough to tell him of my contacts back in London so there would be no suspicion when they called. I also mentioned that we had met some Sicilian Crime Boss at a fundraiser in Venice who had taken a liking to Mirium.

Sleeping was out of the question. I had the windows open for air, but the night was even more humid than usual. I couldn't stop thinking of Mirium, going over and over in my mind how her abduction could have occurred and what more, if anything, I could have done to save her.

I kept having visions of Mirum bound and gagged in a chair in a dark, musty room somewhere, all alone, frightened, just as I had been the year before when I was in a similar situation when kidnapped by the Irish terrorists back in London. I lay in the bed in a cold sweat, finally getting up to pace around my room. At some point I turned on the shower and slowly stripped off the clothes I had been in all day, which were now drenched in sweat with dirt and blood from the scuff with the kidnapper. I stepped under the warm running water, closing my eyes, hoping the water washing over my face would somehow wash away the nightmare of the day. I turned and felt the spray on my head, like tiny fingers gently massaging my scalp, sending chills down my neck and back. For a brief moment, I lost myself in the feeling, then the thoughts of Mirium returned, and I pounded my fist against the wall again and again in the acute agony of frustration and helplessness in the situation.

Ladden woke me from my daze in the early hours of the morning. He had gotten word that the police had a lead from the man I had helped apprehend and were going to a warehouse in a Rome suburb. It was still dark. When we got to the address, the police had it surrounded. We saw the kidnapper's' dark van under a shed roof at the end of the building. A team of men slowly and silently entered the building through a side door that was ajar. After what seemed like an eternity, we heard shouts and gunfire. The police outside hold us back as we tried to run toward the sounds. We are fearing the worst. We heard "man down" over the radio and the cop next to us grabbed his radio to call for an ambulance. We heard more shots fired as we held our breath. The next words we heard on the radios are, "She's here. We've got her. She's drugged, but unharmed!"

The ambulance attendants brought the wounded officer out on a stretcher, and as they were passing us, I felt a gratitude that bordered on love for this man. He had taken a bullet trying to save the woman I love. I stopped the attendants and just said "Thank you!" as tears began to well up in my eyes. He gave me a weak smile and they continued on their way. I turned towards the building as they were wheeling Mirium out in a chair. They had an IV hooked up to her and she was somewhat awake but in a daze. I ran to her side and the attendant put a handout to slow me down and give her some space. I tenderly touched her shoulder and gave her a kiss on the forehead. She gave me a smile that reminded me of a very drunk young lady in a bar. I couldn't help but smile and give a slight chuckle. I wished I had a camera. They took her to a nearby hospital for observation and to sleep off the drug. I stayed by her side in a chair all night.

When they woke her up in the morning to draw some blood and check that she could leave, she looked tired and a bit bedraggled from her experience. Her eyes lit up when she saw me. She looked me in the eye and said, "How are you?" and then murmured "I saw you pounce on that tall man with the gun".

20

Leave it to the Pros

When we returned to our hotel, we had a message from Captain Giovanni. He had heard of our tragic incident and was hoping that we could meet with him that afternoon.

We also had a call from Michael Ladden that he had a good tip from Yuri that there was a restorer's shop in Cesarina, Rome that had a bit of a reputation for disguising paintings prior to movement for private sales. Michael was going to look into that a bit more before visiting the shop.

We left a message for Michael that we were going to meet with the Director again, to see what he had to say, and we would call him when we finished there.

As we entered the captain's reception area, one of the detectives barged in ahead of us and blurted out in a loud voice. Great news! "We just got a lead on a location in Cesarina that may have received the painting. It's a dealer that has been under suspicion for trafficking stolen art." I was discreetly watching the lieutenant during this announcement, to observe his reaction. He briefly closed his eyes and frowned as if annoyed by the detective's lack of discretion and exuberance at being the one to deliver this great news. He took a deep breath before opening his eyes, his face brightened as if ecstatic about the news, then he turned to us, looking thrilled. "This is indeed great news! One step closer to retrieving your valued painting. But before we get ahead of ourselves and start counting on our good fortune, be aware that these things move around quickly so as not to allow time for the authorities to catch up. The painting may be on the move again, even as we speak. That will be all, Lieutenant." "Good recovery" I thought to myself as I glanced at Mirium, who was grasping my arm and looking appropriately excited with the news. She returned my glance with a bit of a smirk, like she was sharing my thoughts.

The lieutenant instructed us to return to our hotel and get some rest while he had his men investigate the situation. Mirium started to protest, but I cut in. "Probably an excellent idea." I turned to Mirium and said, "It's been an exhausting trip, physically and emotionally. Let's do as the Lieutenant suggests. This could get dangerous, and I wouldn't want my fiancé in harm's way." with a wink the lieutenant couldn't see. She looked at me in disbelief and hesitated only a second, then put on one of her signature pouts and said, "OK, I guess that would be best. Leave it to the professionals." We said our goodbyes and as we turned to go, we made a point of telling him to let us know the minute he had more information. As we were leaving he commented, "I'm glad to see that you are putting your future bride's safety ahead of your cavalier nature to retrieve the painting yourself." I smiled and nodded. As we exited his office I caught him, out of the corner of my eye, picking up his phone to make a call.

We walked casually out of the building, turned right to get out of sight of the offices, and headed in the direction of our hotel. The minute we were sure that we were out of sight of the lieutenant and his men, we quickened our pace and cut through the St. Andrea Park and headed to the nearest phone. A quick call to Ladden and he was on his way to pick us up. We rode in his car and filled us in on his search for more information regarding the Head of the Bureau. Seemed that Interpol had been investigating him for the past decade but had never been able to pin anything on him. They had been following our Van Gogh case with mild interest with Michael feeding them info as we progressed. Our episode in Bolzano and the pursuant phone conversation that Mirium had overheard brought their full attention and resources to us. This tip, and the apparent connection between the Lieutenant in Venice and the Director, was the pearl in the oyster. They were coordinating with local and state authorities to meet up with us at the shop in Cesarina. They were able to give Michael directions over the phone.

The drive seemed to take forever, though it was only about 20 minutes. Michael's speed got us there in record time. We arrived just moments before the local authorities. They had apparently thought this was a wild goose chase. They had been adamant about what a respected member of the community the owner of the shop was. When asked about the owner, the inspector went on and on about how long he and his shop had been in their town. He had come from Rome, looking for a quiet and safe place to have his business. He described how much good he had done for the community with gracious donations to town events and causes. He insisted that this type of accusation was totally ludicrous.

As we had driven past the building to park along the road, I noticed through a narrow alley between the building and a line of dense vegetation, that the structure went back quite a way, with additions having been added over the years, in typical farmhouse fashion.

Ladden stayed back in the car as back-up. I was glad he offered to do so. I told Mirum to stay with him. Had I told her to stay by herself, she never would have listened. I got out of the car and joined the local inspector, who had come alone. Not quite the show of authority I had hoped for. We went in through the front door, triggering a bright and pleasant-sounding bell over the door.

A look around the shop showed several impressive pieces of art on the walls, mostly originals of lesser known, but still sought after, artists. There were also several bronze and stone statues, probably here to be authenticated. Some empty antique frames, and a section with artist supplies. A diminutive man, probably in his late 60's or early 70's, with spectacles propped low on his nose, appeared through a curtain behind a small counter. He hesitated a moment and seemed a bit confused and concerned when he saw the inspector, as if he were expecting someone else. After the normal pleasantries between the inspector and the shop owner in Italian, including profuse apologies for the intrusion, the inspector presented the appropriate paperwork for the search, etc. There were several glances in my direction during which the owner seemed increasingly nervous. He seemed to regain his composure as he was introduced to me and managed a warm smile and handshake. His name was Alessandro, he spoke fluent English and he was 'only too glad' to show us around his humble shop. As he put it, "There is not much to show. We are a very exclusive shop that deals with high value, rather than volume."

He proceeded to show us the pieces he had in the showroom, stopping to describe, in detail, each piece, almost as if he were stalling. We politely requested to move on to the rest of the shop, acknowledging how proud he was of his collection, and rightly so, it was indeed impressive. He pushed the curtain open for us to enter a small room in the back. At first glance, it looked like you would expect at a small shop that dealt in fine art and did some restoration work. It had the aromas of paints and clay and even an area for welding to repair metal sculptures. There was a table and chairs in the centre, and a rather muscular man with short hair and equally as short neck, sitting there, playing solitaire. There was a holster and 45 close to his chest. He didn't move, except to glance up at us and then continue his game. A questioning look at the owner prompted a response. "We have many very expensive pieces of art here. A little protection is needed." Guido, say hello to our guests. Without even giving us a look, he grunted without missing a card. "Guido is not much on conversation, but I feel more secure with him here." I had the impression, from the frown on the inspector's face, that he had not known about the presence of this 'security' previously.

"You see, inspector, there is nothing here but a small storeroom." "Too small" I muttered. "Where does that door go?" I asked aloud, pointing to a door off of the back of the room. "Oh, that's just the bathroom." He dismissed. I moved toward the door, and he quickly said, "That's not meant for public use! It is not kept clean. You really don't want to go in there!" As I said, "Humor me", I noticed the man in the chair shifted his weight towards getting up and the inspector's hand moved ever so slightly towards his gun.

I opened the door, against the quibbling of Alessandro, and had to agree, this was not fit for public use, or for use by anyone for that matter. It appeared to be nothing more than a bathroom, but I was remembering the view I had from the road, and I was certain there was more than met the eye. I stepped back from the open door and my eye caught a stream of light coming from under a portion of the wall in the storeroom to the right of the bathroom. Without a word I began to move an easel in front of that section of wall. The man at the table was instantly on his feet, drawing his gun. The inspector simultaneously pulled his out in a face-off. At the same moment, the director appeared through the curtain, also with a gun drawn.

"My, my, what have we here? Mr. Hardigan. Didn't I tell you to leave this to the authorities. Now look what you've done. At least you didn't drag your lovely fiancée here with you. You just can't keep your nose out of this, can you. Why couldn't you have just died, as we thought you had, up in Bolzano. Now you've dragged our esteemed Inspector Leo into this mess, as well. By the way, Alessandro, you are outnumbered. Please, your gun."

The Inspector looked around, assessing the situation and slowly handed his gun over to the Director.

Giovanni stood, looking down at the floor, shaking his head and thinking. After a moment, he directed Guido to open the concealed door to the rest of the building. I bet Mr. Hardigan would love to see his precious van Gogh one more time before he dies. Guido opened an electrical panel in the wall and flipped a switch. The section of wall I had seen began to move up, leaving an opening into a brightly lit and rather modern looking workroom in the back of the building. There appeared to be shelving surrounding the opening on the other side. The Director motioned for me to proceed first, with him right behind me. The leading edge of the shelf was easily within my reach. As I passed through, I turned to compliment the Director on his little operation here. He said, "keep moving." My response of "As you wish" was accompanied by a glance and almost imperceptible nod to the inspector behind him. Instead of turning to continue, I jumped up and grasped the edge of the shelf, bringing my knees up and jabbing my feet into the Director's chest before he could react. As he went toppling over, he fired off a random shot that barely caught me in the left arm. The Inspector sidestepped and grabbed his gun. At that precise moment, Ladden, who had been keeping out of sight behind the curtain, but able to see what was happening, emerged and Guido turned to fire on him. Landon was ready and got a shot off first, disarming and injuring Guido's arm. The Director had returned to his feet and tried to bolt past me. The Inspector fired at his leg, taking him down. Mirium, who had also been outside, hearing all of these shots, came running in a moment later and stood in shock with the curtain drawn, at the scene before her.

The front bell rang, and Mirium spun around, and her hands shot up in the air as she yelled "Don't shoot" in Italian. Ladden and the Inspector had guns aimed and ready. Mirium moved aside, keeping the curtain drawn. A muzzle of a rifle came through the opening, along with one word, "Carabinieri". Michael and the inspector immediately dropped their weapons and we all put our hands in the air. It would have been tragic to get shot by the people we had called for help. It took a moment or two for the state police to sort through the scene, with the Director chiming in about his innocence. But between the photos the police had, a few calls on the radio and everyone's ID's, we were finally free to 'move around the cabin' so to speak. The local inspector could not stop apologizing for doubting our story. We continued down the stairs into the back room and found several easels set up with freshly painted canvases. We were afraid to touch them, afraid we might damage them. The police took over the scene and suggested that we could leave. They assured us that those paintings would not leave their site. We waited until the arrival of an art expert from

Rome, one whom the police deal with on a regular basis. He was able to remove some of the fresh paint and confirm that these were indeed the missing paintings. It seemed like Mirium, Michael and I were holding our breath forever, as we all exhaled in relief. Mirium began to cry tears of relief, as she fell into my arms for support. An armored car showed up to transport the paintings to a secure location, until they could be restored and returned to their vault in Lausanne.

21

Wrap it Up

Giovanni's temporary replacement had some papers for Mirium to sign for security, recovery, and restoration fees, and of course for taxes. The poor gentleman seemed devastated at the turn of events and humiliated that this could possibly have happened. We set an appointment for the next day, to deal with paperwork. We also had signed off for Sotheby's secure transfer to London once the painting was restored. We were told this would take about a month. Sotheby's would then let us know when it would be up for auction, telling us that many of the state and national museums would wish to acquire and exhibit it. Mirium just wanted to get this all over with and go home. Her lawyer had flown in to review all of the documents before she signed anything. The bank also had a representative there to advise her.

With some difficulty, we found a quiet café where we could sit and catch our breath a bit. We needed to be able to talk in private. Now that the painting had been recovered and would be heading off to auction, while we didn't know exactly what it would fetch on the auction block, we knew it would be a considerable sum of money. Mirium had to decide how to allocate that money. She sat down opposite me, putting her elbow on the table in front of her, reaching her hand up, closing her eyes for a moment and resting the bridge of her nose between her thumb and forefinger. She took a long, deep breath and let it out slowly, allowing her neck and shoulders to relax and her mind to focus. I could almost hear her mind ticking away, mentally checking off the options she had been mulling over, moving each option up and down in priority along the list and leaving some options open for new endeavors.

She had always been a staunch supporter of women in society. She had donated to and volunteered for various women's groups in London, as well as overseas. She had helped local groups and families both with moral support and with her checkbook. Now, with several million anticipated from the sale of the paintings, she would continue that work through a new foundation. She would also contribute more to the East London Orphanage for children, through continuing to be a patron and now a wealthy benefactor.

Back at our hotel we were relaxing when Mirium said, "My sister wants to come to the wedding." I said, a bit astonished, "I didn't know you had a sister!" "Yes, she lives in Coventry with a charming husband and two children". "I said that would be great". We wanted a very quiet ceremony at the small local 15th century chapel near her house and a simple, but elegant reception at the estate. I called Frank and brought him up to speed, invited him and Lucy to the wedding and asked for him to be my 'best man' on the day. He seemed genuinely surprised and honored to have been asked and readily agreed. He mentioned that Michel had been training with the British National team and missed me. He also said that Yuri was hosting a 'Celebration Luncheon and Cruise' on his yacht to celebrate Michel being selected for the British National team. Yuri was uncharacteristically emotional about his nephew's success in a field outside of the family business. Frank added something about an exhibition match in the Caribbean in the fall, but I honestly didn't pay much attention. At the mention of the Caribbean, my mind immediately went on walkabout with a vision of Mirium, Frank, Lucy and me on a beach, sipping cocktails.

We decided to take a private jet back to Winston Gardens. We pledged, with a toast of champagne, that we would fulfill the 'legend of the Trevi Fountain' and return to Rome soon. We still had to see the Vatican, the Sistine Chapel and St Peter's Basilica.

Despite being exhausted, emotionally and physically we were not about to disappoint Yuri. We showed up on Saturday dressed informally. Of course, Mirium, as usual, looked magnificent in her beige slacks, pink blouse, and Pierre Cardan sandals. As we stepped on board the party had already started and everyone looked her way. She was used to this, but I was not. I had that frequent sense of privilege at having her at my side.

Yuri quickly came across to us with Michel in tow, welcomed us on board and had one of his waitresses from the club and us champagne. Pretty soon Yuri introduced us to the throng, making it clear we were his special guests. Yuri looked the part in his white Saville Row suit, white shoes, and tie. This was indeed a special occasion.

After a few moments he brought his nephew forward and announced how proud he was that Michel had made the British team. He would now play Davis Cup and go to the Olympics for Britain. He publicly thanked me for helping Michel. I then made a short speech, focusing on how Michel had developed and how proud we were of not only his tennis accomplishments but also how he had recently matured into a fine ambassador for his country.

I reflected back to my recent Buddha teachings that say: "that we are living an illusion – that each person is a mosaic, constantly shifting and changing, that our own actions and thoughts shape our existence". I turned to Michel and said: "it's all up to you – make the most of what you have and what you do. Fill each moment with the best things… seize your moment".

22

Life is Good

I was sitting poolside enjoying the early morning cool breeze. Mid July temperatures can be delightful in England, although the humidity can be uncomfortable. It was a good time to run over the last couple of months in my mind. While there had been months of investigation into Roger Randall's murder, the police had not yet produced any hard and fast evidence that would allow for an arrest in the case. I had found out, in talking to his brother, that Roger was on Lithobid, amongst other drugs and supplements. He often had anxiety attacks before his matches, including before our match on Centre Court. No wonder he was so animated, he was on drugs! The Italian and Swiss police wrapped up the theft of the paintings, bringing a large organization of rare art thieves for the black market to justice. Most of the paintings were recovered, with the exception of two smaller paintings that were easily passed off after the theft, no doubt now hanging in some private collector's office. News coverage was kept to a minimum, the art community preferring to keep the whole matter quiet. They feared it would plant a seed in the mind of other art thieves. They did say that Mirium's kidnapping was just a distraction to buy time for the painting to be moved again.

The Bank of Lausanne compensated Mirium generously for her inconvenience and their mistakes, to avoid any lawsuits and any adverse publicity. Mirium had an authorized copy made of her Van Gogh and had it mounted prominently in the large reception room of her house. It proved to be a great talking point at her charity luncheons and cocktail parties. It looked like the real thing! Her guests were green with envy. As for me, I had an amazing future to look forward to. I still had the yen for travel and adventure in my Australian blood, which complemented the strong and independent woman I was about to marry. Was I now ready to settle down with Mirium and help her manage her estate and her new foundation? With the promise of a never boring woman at my side, the answer was a resounding, "Yes!"

Mirium stepped out of the house, ready for her morning swim. As she passed out of the shadow from the house, the sun behind her gave an otherworldly effect of a goddess stepping from her world into mine. I rose and met her, taking her into my arms for a lingering good morning kiss, as the memories of the past months melted into the anticipation of our future together.

About the Author

Dr. David Staniford has been a tennis professional for more than forty years. A native of Sydney, Australia, he began his teaching career in the Australian outback. Coached by the legendary Australian Davis Cup coach, Harry Hopman, David was a former number one player at the University of Oregon. An outstanding Australian junior tennis player he studied at Sydney Teacher's College and the University of New South Wales. He went on to become an expert in movement analysis, studying at University of Oregon, and the University of London. He has taught and coached players at the University of Oregon, Illinois State University, Brock University in Ontario, Canada, Newberry College, and Marquette University.

His course, 'A Movement Approach to Sports Skills' has been taught in many countries. He teaches and consults with players, teams and coaches on movement and skills technique. He continues to conduct tennis clinics and camps around the world. Several of his players have played Davis Cup for their countries. His books include Natural Movement for Children; Kendall Hunt, Natural Tennis, second Edition; Stipes with John Boaz. Good Strokes for Senior Folks; The New You Publishing and his first fiction novel, Murder at Wimbledon; Fulton Book . He continues to write articles for professional magazines. Presently he is the Tennis Professional at Savannah Lakes Village (SLV), a master-planned, community in McCormick, South Carolina, where he has inspired league play for the residents and taken teams to both state and national competitions, and continues to run clinics and offers leassons. David has made tennis his life, and in return it has afforded him many once-in-a-lifetime experiences.